Blue Wide Sky

Blue Wide Sky

Inglath Cooper

Fence Free
Entertainment, LLC

Contents

First love. . . forever love.

Sixteen-year old Gabby Hayden wasn't the kind of girl who gave a hoot about boys. She had a few real loves. Water-skiing, going out on Smith Mountain Lake with her dad and her dog. Anything else ranked a distant second. Until the summer smart, caring, gorgeous Sam Tatum gave her his heart. It had been the most wonderful time of her life, lazy days hanging out at the dock, skinny-dipping at midnight, staring up at the stars from the back of Sam's truck.

They are planning their future together when Sam's father is transferred to South Africa. Devastated, Gabby and Sam promise to wait for each other until he returns for college. But lonely and angry, Sam makes a mistake that will change the course of both their lives.

Years later, an unexpected diagnosis brings Sam home to his parents' house on Smith Mountain Lake where he believes he can find peace and acceptance. What he finds, however, is the girl he once loved, now a woman unwilling to lose him again, a woman who will make him realize that both love and life are worth fighting for.

Published by Fence Free Entertainment, LLC

Cooper, Inglath
Blue Wide Sky / Inglath Cooper
ISBN – 978-0-9862825-2-2

Fence Free Entertainment, LLC
Fence.free.entertainment.llc@gmail.com

Books by Inglath Cooper

Blue Wide Sky
Rock Her
Crossing Tinker's Knob
Jane Austen Girl
Good Guys Love Dogs
Truths and Roses
A Gift of Grace
RITA® Award Winner John Riley's Girl
A Woman With Secrets
Unfinished Business
A Woman Like Annie
The Lost Daughter of Pigeon Hollow
A Year and a Day
Nashville: Part Eight – R U Serious
Nashville: Part Seven – Commit
Nashville: Part Six – Sweet Tea and Me
Nashville: Part Five – Amazed
Nashville: Part Four – Pleasure in the Rain

Nashville: Part Three – What We Feel
Nashville: Part Two – Hammer and a Song
Nashville: Part One – Ready to Reach
On Angel's Wings

Reviews

"Truths and Roses . . . so sweet and adorable, I didn't want to stop reading it. I could have put it down and picked it up again in the morning, but I didn't want to." – **Kirkusreviews.com**

On Truths and Roses: "I adored this book...what romance should be, entwined with real feelings, real life and roses blooming. Hats off to the author, best book I have read in a while." – **Rachel Dove, FrustratedYukkyMommyBlog**

"I am a sucker for sweet love stories! This is definitely one of those! It was a very easy, well written, book. It was easy to follow, detailed, and didn't leave me hanging without answers." – **www.layfieldbaby.blogspot.com**

"I don't give it often, but I am giving it here – the sacred 10. Why? Inglath Cooper's A GIFT OF GRACE mesmerized me; I consumed it in one sitting. When I turned the last page, it was three in the morning."

– MaryGrace Meloche, Contemporary Romance Writers

5 Blue Ribbon Rating! ". . .More a work of art than a story. . .Tragedies affect entire families as well as close loved ones, and this story portrays that beautifully as well as giving the reader hope that somewhere out there is A GIFT OF GRACE for all of us." — **Chrissy Dionne, Romance Junkies 5 Stars**

"A warm contemporary family drama, starring likable people coping with tragedy and triumph." 4 1/2 Stars. **— Harriet Klausner**

"A GIFT OF GRACE is a beautiful, intense, and superbly written novel about grief and letting go, second chances and coming alive again after devastating adversity. Warning!! A GIFT OF GRACE is a three-hanky read...better make that a BIG box of tissues read! Wowsers, I haven't cried so much while reading a book in a long long time...Ms. Cooper's skill makes A GIFT OF GRACE totally believable, totally absorbing...and makes Laney Tucker vibrantly alive. This book will get into your heart and it will NOT let go. A GIFT OF GRACE is simply stunning in every way—brava, Ms. Cooper! Highly, highly recommended!" **– 4 1/2 Hearts — Romance Readers Connection**

"...A WOMAN WITH SECRETS...a powerful love story laced with treachery, deceit and old wounds that will not heal...enchanting tale...weaved with passion, humor, broken hearts and a commanding love that will

have your heart soaring and cheering for a happily-ever-after love. Kate is strong-willed, passionate and suffers a bruised heart. Cole is sexy, stubborn and also suffers a bruised heart...gripping plot. I look forward to reading more of Ms. Cooper's work!"
– **www.freshfiction.com**

Accept the things to which fate binds you, and love the people with whom fate brings you together, but do so with all your heart.

~ Marcus Aurelius

sam

You know how there are some things in life that you eventually allow yourself to admit you're never going to do again?

Things that you clung to when you were young with the arrogance that underscored life through your twenties, anyway. Until you hit thirty and that little ping of awareness started up.

Uh-oh. This really might not go exactly like I thought it was going to. No u-turns in sight. Just straight-ahead highway like the North Dakota stretch from Gackle to Beaver Creek where you can see so far in the distance, it looks like you'll just fall off the edge of the Earth if you ever do get there.

At some point along the way, that's what I eventually came to accept about Smith Mountain Lake and my memories of it. That this place and everything I had loved about it as a boy were part of my past, a time long gone, so far behind me that it wasn't possible to ever travel back.

Or at least that's what I would have told myself just a few days ago.

And yet here I am now, behind the wheel of a rented Ford Explorer, headed out of Roanoke down 581 south to 220 and the winding curves that will take me back to the heart of my childhood summers.

The H&C coffee pot and the Dr Pepper 10-2-4 signs, both erected sometime in the 40's, are still here among the downtown highrises. The factoid comes to my brain with my father's voice still attached, and I remember how he'd point them out those first summers when we'd drive in from our DC home, headed for the lake house in our packed-to-the-gills station wagon.

New on the city landscape, though, is the train-shaped museum that is a more recent part of Roanoke's contemporary identity. I had read about it online in the *New York Times* and remember the pang just seeing the city name in print lifted up inside me.

To the left of 581, Mill Mountain looms in the distance, its famous star now modestly dim in the daylight. At night, it glows red, white and blue on top of its post, earning Roanoke its nickname as the star city of the south.

A Starbucks, a Lowes, and a BMW dealership have grown up alongside 220 heading out of Roanoke. It looks vastly different from the last time I was here, and I am suddenly anxious to leave the city limits where the countryside starts to appear in short, more familiar stretches.

But it isn't until I've hit route 40 headed east outside of Rocky Mount that I start to see green pastures, black-and-white Holstein cows grazing slope after slope. Barbed wire alternates with white board fencing; the houses ranging in style from brick ranches to two-story farmhouse structures.

I've hit late afternoon traffic, and a big yellow school bus has cars lined up out of sight behind me. The transplanted Londoner in me itches to blow the horn and wave for the driver to pull over and let us all pass. I suppress the urge, realizing I don't want to be that guy. Not here, where everyone seems content to wait. Where I used to be someone content to wait.

The thought of London brings with it a ping of guilt.

I should give Evan and Analise a call. Let them know where I am.

But I don't have the energy to get over that wall just now. It's possible the kids haven't even missed me yet. Evan's on the fast track of a young career, and Analise is nearing the end of her junior year in boarding school. They are both busy and occupied with their own lives.

For now, I'm grateful for this. At some point, I will have to talk with them, but I can use the time here to figure out how I'm going to do that.

And as for Megan, I don't really owe her an explanation of any kind. Sad, but true, after twenty-three years of marriage. The life we built together wasn't initially mine by choice, but I did commit to it, and even though what we had never felt like the love of a lifetime kind of love, I grew to care for her. I was faithful to her. Odd as it sounds, in some strange way, I am glad that I wasn't the one who caused our marriage to end, and that I don't have that particular guilt to live with.

We're still stopping every quarter mile or so, tired-looking children straggling off the bus with weighted book bags slung across their shoulders. At one stop, an enormous yellow lab dances a happy-to-see-you jig alongside a boy and a girl as they trudge up their gravel driveway.

Ten minutes later, the bus finally takes a right and lumbers on to a smaller state road, black smoke puffing from its exhaust.

The cell phone on the passenger seat rings, and my brother's face pops up.

I swipe the screen and take the call. "Ben," I say, hearing the smile in my own voice.

"Brother!" Ben says. "You on terra firma?"

"Yeah, man, and happy to say so."

"Nice to think there's not an ocean between our phones."

"Agreed," I say.

"It's been too damn long since you graced this country with your presence."

"Yeah, I know. Hey, thanks for arranging to get the house ready."

"Glad to do it. I just wish we didn't have this trip planned. We'd be meeting you there."

"I didn't exactly give you any notice. And hey, I'm proud of you. That's some award you won."

"Good excuse for a free vacation to Hawaii," he says.

"It's a lot more than that," I say.

"You know I would have ditched it to see you."

"I do, but I'll be here when you get back in two weeks," I say, feeling a sudden plummet in my stomach at the words as I realize I really have no way of knowing whether that will turn out to be true. "I'll try to be," I amend quickly.

"Uh-uh. None of that. You will be there," Ben says, adamant. "I want to see you."

"I want to see you too, brother."

"So what prompted the spur-of-the-moment visit?"

I start to make light of the question with some fluff version of an answer, but find that I can't. "Just felt the need," I say, and it's more true than I could ever express.

"Glad to hear it. How's the doc business across the pond?"

"A little crazy these days."

"Copy that," Ben says, and I wonder how it is that my neurosurgeon brother can as convincingly shoot the breeze in truck-stop vernacular as he can lay out the complexities of brain surgery to a room full of surgeons.

"Marie and the kids excited about the trip?"

"Just about over the moon. Marie says I have to learn how to surf."

"There's a mental picture I didn't need."

Ben chuckles. "Hey now, long as I don't forget to sunscreen my bald pate, I should do fine."

"Just get video, okay?" I say, smiling. "Where are you calling from?"

"L.A. flight leaves in a couple of hours." Ben hesitates and then says, "Kids didn't want to come with you?"

I hesitate and do my best to avoid a blatant lie. "They kind of have their own lives now."

"Maybe we can get over there for Christmas this year. Sure would be nice to get everybody together."

The words fall on my ears like glass jars to a marble floor. I feel their crack inside me and offer back a hollow sounding, "Yeah, it would."

"Well, then, let's don't just say it. We'll do it."

In the background, I hear an airport announcement, and then my brother says, "I've gotta run, Sam. I'll give you a call in two weeks. I'll drive out to the lake the weekend we get back."

Part of me wants to stop him from hanging up, to hold onto the first thread of normalcy I have felt in days. I feel an unexpected calm in just hearing my brother's voice, its warmth and familiarity an anchor for the emotions I've been trying to keep my head above. Part of me wants to blurt everything out, let him help me make sense of it the way he used to do when we were kids, and he was the kind of older brother all my friends wished they had.

I've never needed his level-headed common sense more.

But now isn't the time. I don't want to ruin this trip he and Marie have looked forward to. It can wait.

"That sounds great," I answer in an even voice. "It'll be good to see you, Ben."

"You too, Sam. Talk to you soon, okay?"

We hang up on that, and I picture him jogging off through the airport, cracking one of his corny jokes to Marie, who considers it an act of love to always laugh, even when no one else does. I've always thought that was as good a definition for love as any I can think of.

I try to remember in the last years of my marriage a time when Megan and I laughed with each other, or even at each other. And I honestly can't bring one to mind. The stone wall of silence had been erected for so long that laughter seemed like a completely out-of-place notion.

I spot the turn-off just ahead, the smaller paved road that leads to my family's summerhouse. There are no cars in front of me now, and I press the accelerator, anxious to get there.

The houses are fewer and farther between on this

road, the pastures wider and dotted with Black Angus cows and calves. Ahead, I can see Smith Mountain, green and beckoning. I'm relieved that it is still free of houses, that its graceful slopes have not been pocked by development.

I take a left and follow the road at the mountain's base. It winds and narrows until I spot the sign for Hayden's Marina on the right. It's been updated. That's the first thing I notice, its colors muted and appealing as the backdrop for the words:

Boat Slips for Rent, Gas, Grill, Picnic Supplies and More! Turn Here!

I pull off the road and find myself gripping the steering wheel, hard.

Gabby Hayden.

I say her name out loud then, and it sounds odd against the *brrrrr* of the Explorer's engine. I haven't let myself say it in so long that it almost feels like I've committed some kind of grievous faux pas in doing so.

What would I do if she came driving up right now, spotted me sitting here like some kind of dazed stalker?

Twenty-five years have come and gone since we were both those sixteen-year old kids falling in love for the first time.

How is that possible?

A lifetime has unfolded since then. One we have lived without each other. There was a point in my younger life when I never would have believed that was possible. Living without Gabby.

I sit until the sun sinks behind the mountain, and, for the first time since I left England some thirty hours ago, I let myself admit that my trip here is about more than seeking my brother's opinion or seeing this place I've never forgotten.

It is also about seeing the girl that I once loved with ever fiber of my being. The girl I have never forgotten.

You don't choose your family. They are God's gift to you, as you are to them.

~ Desmond Tutu

Gabby

I don't know if there has ever been a day when I've woken up to the kind of sunrise now creeping up behind Smith Mountain and not marveled at its beauty. Even when I was a child, I loved to watch its steady climb from my bedroom window. On spring mornings like this one, it is nothing short of extraordinary.

When I was seven or eight years old, I remember thinking that God must have the sun on some kind of invisible pulley that connected with one of the clouds up in heaven, raising it every morning and lowering it in the evenings. It made sense to me that something that incredible could only be delivered from a place so wonderful that my imagination couldn't do it justice.

One morning when my daddy and I were out fishing on the lake, I'd offered up my theory, and he had explained to me how it really worked. He'd told me how the Earth spins on its axis toward the east, and that's why the Sun and the Moon rise in the east and move westward across the sky. I'd said oh, and he must have sensed my disappointment, because he said, "But you know what, honey, I like your version way better. I imagine the good Lord does too."

I think of that conversation often enough that it's the go-by I've looked to for my own parenting with Kat. Some things are more important than being right.

She's up already, an early bird like me, rolling her wheelchair across the dock flooring to the marina gas pumps where I'm hosing pollen from a customer's pontoon boat seats.

I lean over and she gives me a kiss on the cheek. "The Morgans are going out today?" she asks.

"Yes," I answer, rubbing her silky blonde hair between my fingers. "Susan called last night to see if we could have it ready for them this morning."

"Nice day for it," she says, and I think, as I always do, how mature she is for her ten years. It's there in the calmness of her expression. Her whole demeanor, really, is more that of an adult than a child.

But she's been that way since the day I met her in a Siberian orphanage when she had just turned three years old. Her Russian name is Ekaterina, and she's actually the one who shortened it to Kat.

I can only guess at the life she lived before she came into mine, a life that shaped her unusual maturity. I know bits and pieces about the broken bones she'd suffered as an infant, and the diagnosis that had led her impoverished mother to relinquish her to the orphanage when it became clear she would never be able to meet her daughter's needs.

I know that she was held as little as possible by the caretakers for fear that another bone would break, and that they might somehow be blamed.

I know too that the minute I laid eyes on her, even though I had never seen her before, there was no doubt in my mind that I had come all that way just for her. And that she had been waiting for me.

"I can hose it if you like," Kat says now.

I hand the nozzle to her, and she takes up where I left off, rinsing the green dusting from the boat. The pollen pools in the lake water like a thin coat of paint.

"I'll get our breakfast," I say, and head inside the marina cafe where a host of regulars occupy the wood tables and leather booths. The dress code ranges from bib overalls to Nike golfing shorts and shirts, since our community is a mix of farmers and vacationers. Buck Finley, part of the farmer mix, throws out his usual cheerful good-morning and compliments the coffee.

"Pour you another cup?" I ask.

"Myrtle's taking care of me," he says.

"Always, Mr. Finley," Myrtle Biggs calls out from the kitchen where she is frying eggs on the griddle. She throws me one of her wide grins, her teeth whiter than white against her ebony skin. She's got her hair all fixed this morning, but then it's Wednesday, and she goes straight to choir practice as soon as she leaves here.

"That smells good," I call out.

"Two plates coming up," Myrtle says, flipping the eggs and then buttering two slices of toast. "That child's gonna put us all out of a job," she adds, glancing out the front window at Kat. "She's a worker, that one."

"To the point where I feel guilty about it sometimes," I say.

"Oh, no, don't be doing that. It's who she is. She likes being helpful."

"You're right," I say, because it's true. There's nothing that makes Kat happier than helping. "You had your breakfast, Myrtle?"

"Coming up, right after yours," she says.

"The morning paper is on the table if you want to see it."

"Thanks," she says and slides the two plates across the counter to me.

I take them outside to the picnic table, and Kat rolls over to join me at one end. It's barely seven o'clock, and the air feels cool and clean, the way it does in early May. We join hands and Kat says the blessing. Her prayers are always ones of thanks. For the rain. For warmth. For food and shelter. For peace. She never asks for anything for herself, and if she does ask for something, it's a need she's heard someone else express. Healing for old

Mr. Harrison's arthritis, safety for Myrtle's son who's serving in the military.

Her prayers always make my heart contract in a now familiar way. I think as I often do that she is too good for this world, and I say my own prayer that my daughter's bones will grow strong, that the daily pain in her back will disappear. I know that would require a miracle, because every doctor we have seen has concluded it is something she will have to live with. But I am not too proud to ask.

I tuck into my food while Kat takes a half-hearted bite of toast and cuts up her egg, only to relocate each piece on the plate instead of eating any of it.

"Not hungry this morning?" I say.

"Not really," she says.

I put down my fork. "Everything okay?"

"Yep."

I finish off my plate in a deliberate effort to let her elaborate on that, and when she doesn't, I say, "What's going on, sweetie?"

She's quiet and then, "I've been having those dreams again. When I'm asleep, I think I see her face, but when I wake up I can't remember it."

The conversation is a painful one, for Kat, and for me too, if I'm honest. The dreams started when she was seven, and there have been times when she would go long stretches without having them. In the beginning, she would wake up screaming in fear, and I would lie on her bed, holding her as tightly as I dared while she sobbed as if her heart were breaking.

For a long time, she couldn't put words to what the dreams were about. When she was eight, she began to tell me they took place in the apartment where she had lived with her mother before she'd left her at the orphanage.

I take her hand now and give it a gentle squeeze. "I'm sorry, sweetie."

She shrugs. "Yeah."

We sit, quiet, while four white ducks hover at the edge of the dock, hoping for our leftovers. I toss them the crust from my toast, and Kat tears off pieces of hers and throws it their way.

"Think I'll go ahead and start my schoolwork," Kat says, rolling her chair away from the table.

"Need any help this morning?" I ask.

"Not right now," she says. "It's easy."

This is true. Kat is really smart. She absorbs information, facts, figures, theories with enviable ease, and I am thankful that this part of her life at least is not a struggle.

"I'll come check on you in a bit," I say, while she rolls toward my office just behind the cafe and grill where we keep a computer for her homeschooling. I've thought many times about the benefits for Kat going to regular school, being around other children mainly, but she prefers being here. She'd attended the local public school for kindergarten through second grade and seemed to love it, until one day she'd come home and asked me if I would homeschool her.

The only reason she would ever give me was that she was bored, and, although I know this was true, I suspect there were other reasons that she kept to herself.

Myrtle ambles out of the cafe, stopping to give Kat a kiss on the head. I hear her ask if they're on for their cooking lesson at eleven o'clock, and Kat smiles and says yes. It's a funny thing these two have going. Kat has become a near-expert Italian cook just from watching cooking shows and reading cookbooks and blogs. Myrtle does Southern like nobody's business, and so a couple of times a week, they teach each other a new dish in between breakfast and lunch. Whatever they fix ends up being on the specials board for that day, Fried Grits and Gnocchi Pesto. Gingered Peach Cobbler and Tiramisu. Cornbread Casserole and Spaghetti Bolognese.

They've actually developed a following of sorts, an eclectic local bunch who'd initially complained about all the fancy words they couldn't pronounce and just as quickly became converts who told everyone they knew to come out to Hayden's Marina for the Blue Plate Specials. Never knew what you were gonna get, but it was always worth the trip.

I head back outside and glance over the Morgan's boat, just to make sure she's all ready to go. They're good customers, have been so for a dozen years, never complain, and tell everyone they know who's coming to Smith Mountain Lake about our marina. I've always thought it pays to work a little harder to keep customers like that than spend a bunch of advertising dollars on new ones who might not live up to their standard.

The boat is all but spit-shined, so I move on to the next project, the picnic tables I've been repainting. I decided over the winter to put umbrellas in the center of each of the tables to encourage boaters to stop in for a meal, even when the weather is on the hot side. The umbrellas are bright orange, and I'm covering the tables' former faded gray surfaces with a fresh coat of white paint. The result is cheerful and inviting, exactly what I had been going for.

I get the paint bucket from the nearby storage closet and start on the sixth out of twelve tables, spreading the brush across the surface with long, quick strokes. My daddy taught me how to paint when I was around Kat's age. It became my job to keep the dock pylons, window trims, wood doors and such touched up throughout the year. Daddy always told me if I was going to do anything, to do it right. I had taken pride in showing him that I could.

The window to my office is cracked, and I can hear Kat practicing her Russian. With homeschooling, she is able to do this along with her other subjects, and I'm glad that she has decided to renew her memory of the language.

When I first brought her home, she spoke only Russian, but as she learned English, the Russian began to slip away, and when I had tried to reintroduce it, she'd cried horribly, sobbing so hard I could not console her. I could only guess that maybe hearing the language made her think she would be going back, and so for several years, I left it alone altogether. Sometime last year though, she had asked me if I would find a program for her to relearn the language, and she is picking it back up again with a natural fluency, only with a Virginia accent. I love hearing her pronounce the words with the dialect she has absorbed here.

A flock of Canadian geese land in our cove just out from the dock area. They glide across the water's surface, headed for the grassy area next to the boat slips where they usually spend an hour or two hunting and pecking. They aren't the most popular creatures in this community. People complain about the large amounts of poop they leave behind, but I'm partial to them, I guess. They're beautiful to look at, although what I love most about them is their devotion to their loved ones. If a goose's mate or baby is injured or sick, it will stay and guard it until it gets well or dies.

I don't know any better example of one of God's own creatures living out what it means to love someone or to be a parent.

Kat comes out just before eleven o'clock and says she's done with her schoolwork. Her expression is somber in the way she gets when her back is hurting a lot.

"Need some medicine, sweetie?"

"Maybe so," she says.

We go inside my office where I pull the prescription bottle from the desk drawer, grab a bottle of water from the mini-fridge in the corner and hand a pill to Kat. She swallows it dutifully, even though she dislikes taking the medicine because it makes her sleepy.

We head for the kitchen then where Myrtle has the ingredients for her recipe already assembled on the countertop. "Grits and collards is what I'll be doing today. What're you gonna teach me how to make, Miss Kat?" she asks.

"Pappa di Pomodoro," Kat says casually.

"Say what?" Myrtle shoots back.

"Italian tomato and bread soup," Kat translates.

Myrtle harrumphs in the way she always does when these two exchange their recipe of choice. "Well, all right then."

Kat starts to pull ingredients from the cabinets: canned tomatoes, olive oil, cloves of garlic, onion.

I pour myself a glass of iced tea and hang around until my daughter's face is no longer tight with pain, and laughter fills the kitchen. And then I head outside to paint another table.

I am not afraid of storms, for I am learning how to sail my ship.

~ Louisa May Alcott

Kat

Myrtle is one of those people who just make life brighter because she's around you. She takes her cooking as seriously as I take mine, but we do plenty of joking around when we're in the kitchen. Only today, I don't feel like laughing as much as I usually do.

"Do I need to make you one of my coconut cream pies to get a smile out of you, child?" she asks, while I'm sautéing onion and garlic in a pan.

"I wouldn't complain if you did," I say.

She puts her hands on my shoulders and turns me to face her, taking the wooden spoon from my hand and placing it on the counter. She looks in my eyes and says, "You having those dreams again?"

I start to deny it, but it wouldn't do any good with Myrtle. I nod.

She turns off the stove, ushers me over to a barstool at the counter and says, "Sit. Let's chat a bit."

"I'm okay, Myrtle."

"Tell me what you're worried about, sweetie."

I look down at my hands, twist them for a few seconds and then say, "I keep dreaming that something is going to happen to Mama. And I won't have a family anymore."

Myrtle looks at me for a long moment, her eyes welling with tears. "Oh, sweet girl." She reaches out and pulls me into her arms, saying, "No one could blame you for worrying about it. Not with everything you've already experienced in this life. But your mama is a healthy young woman who has no intention of going anywhere that doesn't include you."

"Things happen to people all the time though," I say. "They get sick. Or in car wrecks."

"This is true," Myrtle says. "But that's where our faith comes in. We have to trust that God's got it all worked out. How else would your mama have come all the way over there in Russia to get you? That's just nothing but a miracle."

I nod because I have to agree. "I just wish I would stop having the dreams."

"With time, honey, I think that will happen. Fear can work on us, even when we're sleeping."

"I guess so."

"But here's what you need to know. Your mama loves

you more than you can even begin to imagine. Every time you start to feel worried, just think about that."

I nod and lean over to give her a hug. "Thanks, Myrtle. I love you."

She hugs me back, extra tight. "I love you too, sweetie. Now don't we have a competition to finish?"

"We do."

She slides off her chair and says, "Don't be thinking I'll be cutting you any slack just because we took a time out."

I smile. "I won't, Myrtle."

Holding on to anger is like grasping a hot coal with the intent of throwing it at someone else; you are the one who gets burned.

~ Buddha

sam

I wake up to what sounds like American Idol for blue jays, carried out by a series of songbirds who continue to one up the previous competitor in volume if not substance. The show started at six a.m., and at seven, I shake off the jet lag and head for the shower.

The house is showing its age, or rather lack of use, and the pipes are no exception. They rattle in protest at my request for function, churning and chugging before complying with a reluctant surge and then a steady, if unimpressive, stream.

Ben and his family visit a couple of times each year, but other than that, its care has been left to a local couple who check in once a month and make any obvious house repairs that are needed.

Ben has tried to get me to agree to sell a number

of times, but it wasn't something I could ever consider beyond an initial admission to practicality.

My attachment to this place is a cord to the past, and I have never conceded to cutting it.

Standing here before the mirror I had used to brush my teeth and wash my face as a boy, I am grateful that something inside me had never let me do it.

Being here is the first thing that has felt right to me in a very long time.

Downstairs, I make coffee in a retro pot, watching the brown liquid bubble up through the glass knob on its top. The coffee is good, and I sit down at the walnut kitchen table my mother had refinished after finding it at a flea market. She loved to hunt through the local sales when we were boys, dragging Ben and me along with her on a Saturday morning when we wanted to be out on the lake fishing or skiing. It was the last thing we wanted to do, but I came to appreciate her eye for a good piece, a pine pie safe, a cherry bookcase, a set of ladder-back chairs.

Each of those finds still has their place in this house, and it is like having some small piece of her in each room.

Pulling into the driveway last night, I felt an overwhelming sense of loss for my mother and my father. They've both been gone now for more than ten years, their deaths separate and unrelated, his in an early morning car accident on the way to work, hers to a stroke one summer afternoon when she'd been weeding in her garden.

I miss who they had been here, carefree and determined to put the responsibilities of regular life behind them for the duration of a visit. I know now how hard it had been to do that, and I'm grateful they'd carved out this escape for themselves and for Ben and me.

I finish two cups of coffee, and feeling more like myself, set about opening up the house. I raise the windows on the first floor, breathing in the spring air and the scent I instantly remember as unique to this lake, some combination of white pine and fishing boats, just-mowed grass and mountain laurel.

The day has dawned perfectly. I step out onto the front porch and its wide-open view of the lake at the edge of the yard.

Our main house was in Washington, DC, but my parents had purchased this place as a summer home when larger lots could be bought here for nearly bargain prices. The house and surrounding land total thirty acres, and since I had recently heard the going price for a three-quarter acre building lot, I can only imagine the property's current market value.

The view from here is a wide-water one that stretches out to meet the foot of Smith Mountain in the distance. In my adult life, I've been fortunate enough to see a good number of beautiful places, but none outdo this one.

Boats are already buzzing about, three fishing boats, a pontoon and a MasterCraft with an early morning skier cutting back and forth across the wake.

I head for the dock, itching suddenly to get out on the water. Our old boat hangs in its slip, a wooden Chris-Craft that my father had taken extraordinary pride in. I turn on the lift switch, and the boat begins to lower. The key is in the same place where we always kept it, beneath a storage trunk inside the dock house.

I grab some rags and a bottle of Windex and then start to unsnap the boat's cover, pulling it off to find the interior surprisingly clean. I touch up a few areas the birds have gotten access to, and then start the boat. It complains a bit at first, but then sputters to life, the engine's ch-ch-ch sound making me remember how proud my dad was of this boat and the pleased way he would smile when it started right up.

"Pay for quality, you get quality," I'd heard him say more times than I could count. I have to admit, in this case, it is true, considering the boat's age.

I back out of the slip and then glide from the cove, letting the engine warm up before I accelerate across the water, the wind whipping at my hair, the cool, clean air rejuvenating.

I check the gas gauge, see that it says half a tank and open up the boat, one channel marker to the next, taking in both the familiar and no longer familiar at all. The developments are the new thing, clusters of expensive houses having replaced most of the farms I remember as a boy.

Some of the original houses are still here, but they are few and far between. I feel a pang of regret for all the change, even as I acknowledge its inevitability. I drive all the way to the end of the Roanoke River and then swing back, eyeing the gas gauge and its already dramatic drop. Fuel economy isn't this boat's selling point.

I never even consider looking for a place other than Hayden's Marina, driving straight there as if this has been part of my agenda all along. I guess on some level it has, even if it's gone unacknowledged until now.

What's the likelihood that she would still be there anyway? True, the name on the road-front sign had been the same, but a lot of times, even when businesses are sold, the new owners keep the old name because of its recognition factor.

I realize I am arguing myself into a corner. I'll get the gas and be on my way, regardless of who's there or who's running the place. But even as I pull up to the pump, my heart has started a heavy thumping, and my hands begin to sweat.

A teenage boy comes out to help me tie up the boat. "Hey man, how's it goin'?" he asks.

"Good," I say. "Fill her up?"

"Sure thing. Cafe's got some good food if you're hungry."

"Thanks. I'm okay."

He pops off the gas cap and begins filling the tank. I step out onto the dock, running a hand across the back of my neck.

The bones of the place are the same, but major renovation has been done since I was last here. The cafe area has been expanded, and there's a sunroom seating area to one end that looks cheerful and inviting. The same is true of the outdoor tables, at least those that have a fresh coat of paint, the others waiting their turn.

A young girl in a wheelchair rolls out of the cafe. I step forward to hold the door open for her while she maneuvers through.

"Thanks," she says and gives me a shy smile.

"You're welcome," I say, the odd thought that she might be Gabby's child hitting me, but I quickly dismiss it. She looks nothing like Gabby. I glance around to see if there are any parents waiting for her. I don't see anyone except for the boy pumping my gas.

"Hey, Kat," he calls out to her, "how about throwing me that towel from my chair?"

"Only if you agree to eat a dish of Myrtle's collard greens."

"For what?" he shoots back.

"Because she thinks nobody liked her dish today."

"Hate to say it, but I'm gonna be one of them."

"Collards and what?" I ask.

The girl looks at me. "Grits."

"Interesting," I say. "I'll try some."

Her smile is instant and genuinely pleased. She picks up the boy's towel and throws it to him with the comeback, "There are a few gentlemen left around here."

She then waves me inside the cafe. I look at the boy and shrug in apology, but he just grins as if he's used to it.

I hold the door for her again, while this time, she wheels back inside the cafe. The place is surprisingly appealing with walls the color of butterscotch. But it's the smells that I'm sure keep the customers coming back. I can't decide which are more predominant, roasted garlic and rosemary or butter and hot biscuits.

My stomach does an unexpected rumble just as the girl calls out to a woman in the kitchen. "Myrtle, you got an order of the grits and collards left back there?"

"Or two," she says, with enough rancor that I'm uncertain exactly what it is these two have going.

"Good, we have a customer asking for it."

Myrtle perks up instantly. She peers around the corner to look at me. "You saw it on the board outside then?"

I start to say something, but the girl answers, "Of course he did. How else would he know?"

Myrtle smiles at me, and I can see she's more than

aware that she's being hoodwinked. "How else indeed?" she asks. "Would you like that for here or to go, sir?"

"To go is fine," I answer.

The door swings open, and I glance over my shoulder just as Gabby Hayden walks in.

I've read plenty of books, watched plenty of movies that depict this very moment, where two people who had once loved each other come face to face for the first time in many years. And I have to say, I don't think any of them depicted it in a way that I could ever have understood before this moment.

My chest is suddenly so tight, air can't find its way into my lungs. My head feels as if all the blood has rushed up and is threatening to pound its way out. I'm sure it only takes a second or two to register any of this, but a day's worth of hours could have passed for all I know before I finally manage a strangled sounding, "Gabby."

"Sam." She lets the door go in surprise, and it clatters shut, breaking the awkward silence that has settled over the cafe.

"You two know each other?" Myrtle offers up from the kitchen. "Shoulda told me, Gabby, you'd met someone with such fine tastes."

"He's ordering Myrtle's grits and collards, Mama," the young girl explains.

I register the word Mama and realize Gabby is this girl's mother after all.

Gabby looks from one of us to the other, as if she's sure she's walked into some kind of reality warp, and none of this could be happening.

"Yeah," I say. "It sounds good."

"Kat, could you give Timmy a hand at the pumps?" she says to the girl. "He's gotten the on/off lever stuck again."

"Sure," Kat says, and then looking at me, "Thanks for coming in."

"You're welcome," I say.

Some of the pressure seems to leave the room with her retreat. Myrtle puts a to-go container on the counter and just as quietly disappears from view.

Gabby and I stare at each other, words completely elusive.

"How are you?" I finally manage.

Judging from her expression, the question is as lame as I thought it to be. "Fine," she says. "And you?"

"Good," I answer, and then wonder what she would say if I told her the truth.

"What are you doing here?" she asks, running a hand through her hair, still long and silky, still that beautiful shade of blonde.

"I'm spending some time at my parents' old place."

"Ah," she says, as if that explains everything when I am sure she is wondering why now, after all this time?

"I've been out on the lake. Just needed to fill the

tank." I reach for the to-go container. "Mine and the boat's."

Her smile is tepid, and I wonder how I could have managed such an asinine comment. She steps to the register and waves a receipt at me. "This is for your gas. I'll add on the special." She bangs a few keys on the register and says an amount.

I hand her my credit card, and we wait in silence for the machine to rule accept or reject. Its ding is positive, and she hands me back the card.

"Nothing to sign," she says.

"Thanks."

"Thanks for coming in," she adds, and with that she walks through the cafe to the kitchen and is gone.

I stand, shocked I guess, by the dismissal. But then what had I expected? Tearful admissions of how glad she is to see me, remorseful apologies for all the letters she had sent back to me, unopened. Any of that would have been ridiculous, considering, but still, I have a hard time making my feet move. Maybe it's pride that finally forces me to do so, carrying my plastic container of collards and grits with me to the boat where the dock boy — Timmy — is waiting with a wide grin.

"Thanks for taking that hit, sir," he says, glancing at the box in my hands.

"Can't be that bad," I say.

"I'm just not a collards kind of guy," he confesses,

still grinning. He hustles over to untie the rope from the stern, and then jogs to the front for the other.

"Thanks," I say.

"No problem!"

He's about to push the boat away from the dock, when Gabby calls out, "Timmy, wait."

He glances up and says, "Yes, ma'am?"

She jumps onto the boat and says to him, "I'll be back in a few minutes." And then to me, "Drive."

Neither Timmy nor I say a word in response. He steps back, and I ease the boat forward out of the cove.

She says nothing until we are far enough away from the marina that no one can hear. She then points at an inlet several hundred yards away and says, "There, please."

I still say nothing, just steer the boat in the direction she has indicated for me to go. We're there in two minutes, and I cut the engine far enough out from the shore that we won't immediately float in.

When I turn around, she is standing at the back of the boat with her hands on her hips, glaring at me with near fury on her face. "Seriously??!!"

I don't know what to say to this, so I choose continued silence, which seems to suit her because she picks up with, "All these years . . . all this time . . . and you just pop in for grits and collards?"

It is a ridiculous image, and if I weren't witnessing

firsthand the fire in her eyes, I would have laughed. As it is, I say, "Actually, that part was an afterthought."

She stares at me as if I have become something completely unrecognizable to her. "Okay, clearly, I made a mistake in getting on this boat."

I watch in amazement as she steps onto the wood platform just above the motor and makes a neat dive into the lake.

"Gabby!" I call out. "What are you doing?"

She doesn't look back, doesn't answer at all, just swims in swift, clean strokes in the direction of the marina. I can't believe she is actually doing this. Not sure what to do, I crank the motor and pull up ahead of her. "Get in, Gabby. Please. Just let me take you back."

"Go away," she yells, swimming fast and hard, her anger defining each stroke.

I idle alongside her. "And let you get run over by another boat? I'll take you back to the dock. That's all. Gabby, come on. I mean it."

An enormous speedboat roars down the lake straight toward us, its engines wide open. Gabby stops swimming, glances at the boat, then at me, and hesitates as if she can't decide which is the lesser of two evils.

I am the reluctantly chosen winner. I lean out and offer her a hand up the ladder, but she ignores it and climbs in, her shorts and T-shirt soaked and clinging. I stare and then catching myself, swing away to the steering wheel. "I'd offer you a towel, but I don't have one."

"Just take me to the marina," she says, pressing her lips together.

But I point the boat back toward the inlet and return to the spot where we had stopped a few minutes ago.

"Are you kidding?" she cries in a voice that is now more exasperated than angry. "I want to go back!"

"And I'll take you, if you will listen for just a moment."

"What could you possibly have to say that I would want to hear?"

"I'm sorry for showing up like I did. Honestly, I couldn't really imagine that you would be here. That I would see you."

I guess there's enough vulnerability revealed in the admission that she is clearly unsure where to go with it. "You wouldn't understand this is a place I actually want to be," she says.

"I do understand it. I just didn't think luck would ever allow us to cross paths."

"So that's what you were relying on? Luck?"

I shake my head. "That's not what I meant."

"It doesn't matter what you meant, Sam," she says.

"What I meant is that I was hoping you would be."

"Why?" she asks, shaking her head. "After all this time, why?"

It is not a question I can answer fully. Not here. Not

like this. "There are things I want to tell you about what happened after I left here. Things—"

"What could you possibly have to say," she interrupts, furious again, "that would matter in the least? That would make even an ounce of difference?"

"It matters to me, Gabby."

"And why should I care about that?"

"If you'll just give me a chance to—"

"To what? Absolve your guilt? Make yourself feel better finally? I don't think I owe you any such thing, Sam."

"You don't," I agree.

"Then take me back," she says, and this time I can tell that she means it. I start the engine, turning the boat around and letting it pick up speed until we reach the no-wake zone of the marina where we float to the dock under a painful silence.

Timmy catches the boat as we swing in, and Gabby is off before he can offer her a hand. She storms across the dock and disappears around the building without once looking back. It's as if she's rehearsed the action before so that there is no temptation to give in to a glance over her shoulder.

And as I pull out into the cove, I think that here is where we are different.

I look back.

If you love somebody, let them go, for if they return, they were always yours. And if they don't, they never were.

~ Kahlil Gibran

Gabby

I should know better.

But running is the only thing I can think to do that has any shot at pounding this anger out of me.

It feels as if I am literally on fire with it, the heat in my veins acting as fuel for my sprint down old Smith Mountain Road.

There are no cars in sight, and it's a good thing, since the look on my face would probably cause them to think there's a mad woman on the loose.

I keep this up for nearly a mile, until my heart is throbbing so hard I take pity on it and slow my pace. I can barely pull air into my lungs, and my chest hurts as if a small elephant is sitting on it.

I finally concede to a walk, dragging in breaths, and it's only then that the tears start. It's as if a faucet inside me has been turned on, and a waterfall of sobs erupts up and out.

I hate myself for them. Instantly. Completely.

I step off the road into a wooded area and walk through the trees until I come to a giant oak far enough in that passing cars can't see me. I collapse at its base, my face dripping sweat, tears and snot. I lean my head against its hard trunk and cry until the well is dry.

I'm not sure how long it takes, but by the time I'm finished, my heart rate has slowed to something close to normal. A crow caws from a tree limb above me, whether in mockery or sympathy, I'm not sure. I use the jacket tied around my waist to scrub my face free of its mess, and stare up at the blue sky peeking down at me through the trees' limbed canopy.

Of all the ways I might have imagined myself reacting to seeing Sam Tatum again, Hell Hath No Fury isn't one of them. Indifference would have been my emotion of choice, and the only one I would have considered him deserving of.

Instead, I had given him a show that could only be carried out by a jilted lover with twenty-some years of pent-up rage ready to spew at the first opportunity.

I just hope that Kat did not witness any of it.

What was I thinking?

Obvious answer—I wasn't.

I hear a noise behind me, and startled, lean around

the tree trunk to spot a fine-boned doe staring at me, wide-eyed. I sniff. "Hey," I say.

She backs up a step but keeps looking at me, clearly trying to decide whether I am a risk.

"I know. I'm ridiculous."

She chews, and then reaches up for another snack from a young tree's lower limbs, obviously deciding I'm not much of a threat.

I slide around the trunk so I can see her better, and she remains where she is, still chewing.

"He just showed up out of nowhere," I say, looking at the doe. Her ears do a quick dance, back and forth, as if interpreting what I've just said. "Talking to my daughter," I add. "Buying food in my cafe. That's just crazy."

The doe reaches for another leaf or two, blinking her wide brown eyes at me and twitching her white tail.

"Who has that kind of nerve?"

She lowers her head and scratches a place on her leg with her teeth and then shakes her head once, hard.

"Exactly," I say. "I should have just kicked him out altogether. Never exchanged a single word with him. It's like we never knew each other. I mean he looks a lot the same, but I don't know this version at all. I don't want to know this version. I want to remember him the way he was—"

I stop there and realize what I am about to say. Before we didn't love each other anymore.

I put my elbows on my knees and rest my head in my hands. I am talking to a deer. I hear her move then and look up to find her trotting off through the woods away from me.

I don't blame her. I'm beyond pathetic. I sound like the sorest of losers, a woman who never loved another man the way she loved her first love.

But that's me. I never did. And I tried. I wanted to love someone else. I wanted to replace him, erase him. Forget I had ever known him.

There were times in my life when it seemed to work. Stretches where I found someone I had a lot in common with, could laugh with.

Inevitably, I always ended up comparing him to Sam. I had even done so during my short-lived marriage to one of the nicest guys to ever walk the earth. A man I should have been able to love forever. Give myself to completely.

But the truth is there had never been room in my heart for anyone but Sam.

This is the crux of my fury at him.

That he had gotten over me.

And I had never gotten over him.

Maybe, in some way, I have been waiting for this day all along. Waiting for him to come back.

I hate myself all over again for the admission. It sounds so weak, so opposite of everything I try to be. A woman who can take care of herself, who believes in the importance of setting such an example for her child.

And yet, I know it's true.

I *have* been waiting for him to come back. All this time. All these years.

Sitting here now with only the trees as my observers, I decide that maybe there is one reason for me to accept his being here.

So I can finally let him go.

For good.

The wheel is come full circle.

~ **William Shakespeare**

sam

It's nearly dusk when I take a bottle of Cabernet and one of my mom's old jelly-jar glasses out on the front porch. I sit down in a squeaky rocker and decide not to get up until I've finished off the whole thing.

I'd picked it up in France last summer when I'd taken Evan and Analise to Cannes and Saint Tropez on vacation. At twenty-two, Evan had developed a passion for red wine, not so much the taste, thankfully, but the art of making it and the history behind it. He'd picked out this particular one, praising its modest price against its impressive bouquet.

The wine is smooth on my tongue and goes down with a velvety finish, living up to his praise.

Lights from boats out on the lake start to flick on in the growing dimness. I hear frogs in the distance, a chorus of soprano and baritone that makes me nostalgic for the days when my brother and I used to sit out here on summer nights, trying to figure out how many frogs it would take to make such a symphony of sound.

I lean back and close my eyes, the debacle of this afternoon drifting up from the place where I had insisted it stay buried until now.

Once I'd gotten back to the dock, I raised the boat in the lift and stayed busy for a while hosing off the wood decking, sweeping cobwebs from the porch rafters, pretty much any physical thing I could find that would keep me from reliving what was clearly an unfortunate decision on my part.

I never should have gone to the marina.

Had I thought we would just pick up like old childhood friends or something? That all the years since then would discount what I had done? That she would no longer hate me?

Well, if I'd had any hope of that, I have my answer now.

She hates me.

I take another sip of the wine and wait for it to dull the sharp edges of the realization. But for this, the wine has no power whatsoever.

Through the screen door behind me, I hear a knock from the other side of the house. I leave my wine on the floor beside the chair and head through the living room to the back door.

I pull it open to find Gabby standing a few steps away

with her hands in the pockets of her jeans, her expression guarded.

"Hey," she says.

"Hey." I'm too surprised to see her to add anything more intelligent to the greeting.

She looks down once, shifts in obvious discomfort and then forces her gaze to mine. "I owe you an apology," she says.

"You don't," I disagree. "Actually, I owe you one. I shouldn't have come there like that today, Gabby. I really had no right."

"I had no right to act like that," she says, her tone regretful. "I'm really embarrassed."

"Don't be," I say. "You could have hit me. I wouldn't have blamed you."

She smiles then, a quick reflexive smile that feels like it surprises us both. Just that one moment renews my memory of what a beautiful girl she was, what a beautiful woman she now is.

She extinguishes the smile, glances off and then, "Seriously, I'm usually a lot more level-headed than that."

"You don't need to explain or justify anything."

"Well, I just wanted you to know for however long you're here, you're welcome to fill up at the marina anytime. You or your boat."

I smile at this. "You can tell Timmy he's missing out

on those grits and collards. I haven't eaten anything that good in a long time. I actually had it for dinner."

"I'll tell Myrtle. She and my daughter have a competition of sorts going. Kat does Italian, Myrtle Southern. Myrtle gets her feelings hurt if her dish doesn't go over as well."

I stare at her, wanting to say a thousand things, forcing myself down to one. "Your daughter. She's lovely."

"Thanks. She's . . . everything."

It's an interesting word choice, but I can see in the look on her face that it is exactly what she means. All that matters to her.

"I was just having some wine out on the porch. Would you like a glass?"

She considers the invitation as if it has sharp edges attached. Which, of course, it does. We've exchanged pleasantries now, reached the level of civility we would accord old acquaintances. Wisdom would probably dictate leaving it at that.

But I'm not feeling the need to be wise. And I wait in deliberate neutrality while she weighs her decision.

"Just one glass," she says, after a few moments, and I feel as if I have been holding my breath, oxygen now flooding my body.

I hold the door open and wave her inside. I grab another glass as we walk through the kitchen and then the living room. She glances around and says, "It's hardly changed."

"I kind of like that about the place," I say. "There aren't many things you can go back to that are pretty much the same as they are in your memories."

Even as the words come out, I recognize their irony and the direct implication to Gabby and me. I can see in the quick flash of emotion on her face that she too has made the same comparison.

I want to apologize, but don't know how to do so without opening a conversation we are better off avoiding. Still, I am amazed that anything about me has the power to hurt her.

She steps out on the porch and stands at the railing, one hand gripping the top, hard. "It was always a beautiful view here, even at night with the marker lights across the lake," she says.

"Yeah. I think I had let myself forget how much I love it here."

She says nothing, and I wonder if it is possible for us to ever get past this awkwardness. I hand her a glass and pour from the wine bottle.

"That's good," she says, signaling for me to stop pouring. "Virtual teetotaler here."

I set the bottle on the floor and retrieve my own glass, then lean against the railing, putting a few feet of deliberate space between us.

Gabby looks at the glass and says, "I recognize these.

What was that brand of jelly you always liked with your PBJ's?"

I say the name, surprised I remember it, and then, "Mom never liked to throw anything away, so jelly jars became wine glasses."

"Green before green was in," she says.

"She was, actually," I say, maybe realizing it for the first time. "I remember her taking Ben and me out early on Saturday mornings to pick up trash on the side of the road before most people were up."

"Character building too," she says, and we both smile.

We sip our wine, and then she says, "London, right?"

The question catches me off guard, and I say, "London?"

"Where you've been living?"

"Ah." Feeling like an idiot, I add, "Yes. London."

"This is the first time you've been back to the lake since you left?"

"Yes."

"Thought I'd have heard through the grapevine if you had. I've actually run into Ben and his family a few times when they've been down for a visit."

I'm surprised at this. Ben never mentioned it. Maybe he thought it would have been cruel to do so. Part of me is glad that he never did.

"So why now?" she asks.

I take another sip of wine, stalling. "Life changes."

"Is that a statement or an explanation?"

"Both, I guess."

She waits for me to go on, but I can't seem to find words beyond those two.

"Sorry," she says. "It's none of my business."

"No, it's not that. I just—"

"Why isn't your wife with you?"

I can almost hear the words underlying this last question—why are you here with me when you should be with her? "We're divorced," I say.

Surprise flashes across her face, and I can see it is the last thing she expected to hear. "Oh."

"Yeah. I think we both realized it hadn't been working for a long time."

"I'm sorry."

Her question and my answer have altered the atmosphere of the room. There's an instant tension between us that wasn't there previously.

"When—" she starts.

"A year ago," I say.

We're silent for a good long while. I can sense her processing this, as if trying to decide whether it is relevant to her or not. She sets her wine glass down on a nearby table. "I should go."

I should let her. It's the right thing to do. But instead, I say, "Can you stay a while?"

She looks at me, and I can tell she's trying to read beneath the surface of the question. Assess my motive.

The only one I have is a need to look at her a little longer.

"A few more minutes," she concedes.

"Walk down to the lake?"

"Sure," she says, reaching for her glass again, and stepping off the porch onto the grass.

I follow behind her, and then we're side by side, silent all the way to the water.

She steps onto the dock ahead of me, walks to the far edge and sits down, slipping the sandals from her feet and putting them beside her. She rolls up the bottoms of her jeans and sticks her feet in.

"Cool?" I ask.

"Perfect, actually," she says. "Try it."

It's been a long time since I sat on a dock with my feet in the water, but I follow her lead, and then say, "That's cold!"

"Wimp," she says.

"Maybe. But you always were tough."

She drags her feet through the water, cocking her head to one side. "You were the one who went waterskiing in March on your spring break. Not me."

"Without a wetsuit. Can't imagine I was ever that brave."

"I think we were so anxious for the summer to begin, we just couldn't wait."

A whippoorwill sounds across the cove. "I used to love that sound, "I say.

"Summer nights and cookouts, going to bed late and telling ghost stories."

"Exactly. All those things."

We sit for several silent moments like two awkward teenagers looking for something to say that doesn't sound dumb.

"Remember those campouts we used to have here in your yard?"

"Me and Ben and you and Lindsay Turner?"

"Yeah. I never saw Lindsay again after high school. I heard she joined the Peace Corps."

"Did she and Ben ever—"

Gabby gives me a look. "Not by any admission to me."

I roll my eyes. "Figures. I should have known better than to believe Ben."

"What do you mean? Ben was cute."

"Yeah, but he was a dork. Funny, but a dork."

"Maybe to you."

I raise an eyebrow. "What does that mean?"

"It means all the local girls thought he was hot."

"Oh, they did, did they?" I smile, shaking my head.

"They did."

"Glad it never got back to him. It was already hard enough for his neck to support that big head with that big brain."

Gabby laughs. "He was a smart one."

"Add a big ego to his resume, and we wouldn't be able to stand him."

"I hear he's done well. Johns Hopkins neurosurgeon, no less."

"He has. Garnered himself quite a reputation."

"Amazing you both went on to be doctors. Your parents must have been very proud." She hesitates, and then adds, "Ben told me about your work one time when he was here."

"It never had the movie-star quality of his, but I've enjoyed it."

"Hearts are as important as brains, aren't they?"

I shrug. "I just meant that Ben tends to lend whatever he's doing his larger than life persona. He gets invited all over the place to give talks. In fact, they just left yesterday for Hawaii."

"That's great."

"It is," I agree. "I really am proud of him."

She looks at me, and then says, "You said enjoyed."

"What?"

"Past tense. Enjoyed your work."

"Oh," I say, shaking my head. "Symptom of being on vacation, I guess." I sip from my wine glass, suddenly aware of feeling as if I've told her a lie.

"Ah. Out of sight. Out of mind."

A houseboat cruises down the lake with music blasting, and laughter and voices drift out to us. The floating rectangle of light rounds a bend and is soon out of sight, although we can still hear the partying going on.

"Do you mind if I ask about Kat?" I ask.

"What's wrong with her, you mean?"

"That's not what I—"

"She has osteogenesis imperfecta."

"Brittle-bone disease."

"Yes," she says, and I hear the pain beneath the word. "I adopted her from a Siberian orphanage when she was almost three."

"Did you know she had it then?"

"Yes. Or it was the doctors' best guess. But it didn't matter."

I can tell there's more, so I wait.

"I went there to meet a child," Gabby says, after a few moments, "so worried about the right match, wondering if he or she would be able to love me, if I would know how to take care of him or her? I made huge lists of questions to ask—pages, I mean—things I thought I had to know before I could make such a decision. I intended to make sure I had satisfactory answers to each and every one before I let myself decide.

"But then they took me into a room where a tiny girl with blonde hair sat at a table playing with blocks. She had this enormous bow on top of her head. I couldn't take my eyes off her. She looked up at me and said the Russian word for play. And that was it. I never asked a single one of those questions. They no longer mattered. I knew I had met my child."

I absorb everything she's just said. "That's incredible, Gabby."

"I later found out that they never thought I would actually adopt her once I learned about the disease. But they wanted to give her a chance to be considered. No one had ever wanted to meet her before that. The orphanage director was this amazingly kind woman who loved Kat and wanted her to have a good life. She knew they would not be able to afford the kind of medical attention she would need."

When I finally do find my voice, I say, "That's amazing, Gabby. You're amazing."

"Kat is the amazing one. I've learned more from her than I could ever hope to teach her."

"Has she had broken bones since you brought her home?"

"Femur twice. Each arm once."

I wince. "Why is she in the wheelchair?"

"For the past year, she's had pretty much constant back pain because of a disc in her spine. The pain is worse when she walks, so she uses the chair. We've seen doctor after doctor, and the conclusion is that the surgery is too risky."

"I'd love to know more about her case," I say.

She looks at me as if she's wondering whether my request has been made out of politeness or curiosity, but it's neither, and I think maybe she sees this. "Thanks," she says.

There's something in her voice that tells me she's not used to offers of help of any kind. "It must be hard," I say, "handling all of that on your own."

"Sometimes," she says, shrugging. "I just want to do what's right for her."

"She's lucky to have you."

"I'm lucky to have her."

It's enviable, the obvious bond between the two of them, forged I would guess from needs and wants that go beyond the normal. A child with medical issues, even the strongest of families would be challenged by. And a woman who wanted this child with all her heart and soul.

"Did you ever get married, Gabby?" I ask, and the question surprises even me. It's just out there, hanging in the stillness surrounding us, bold as the ebony of the night.

"Yeah," she says. "A long time ago, when I—"

She stops there, and I want her to finish the sentence, somehow needing to hear what had happened. "When you?"

"Didn't know what people need to have between them to last."

It's a big statement. I consider it, and then say, "I've learned something about that myself."

It feels as if we're walking a tightrope here, a misstep to either side bringing a promised topple into things I'm not sure we're ready to talk about.

"I should go," she says.

She's right. I know it, and yet I don't want her to. I suddenly want to know everything there is to know about her life. Even though I'm the last person on earth with any right to. "I'm glad you came over, Gabby."

She puts on her sandals and gets to her feet. I stand up next to her, and we suffer through a few moments of awkwardness, what to say next, me not wanting to move because it will just make her leave sooner.

"I hope you enjoy your stay here, Sam," she finally says.

I hear the finality in this statement, as if she doesn't expect us to see each other again. My mind races with the need to somehow tell her that being here without seeing her doesn't make any sense at all. But I can't. It's too much. Too soon. I feel it.

So I just say, "Okay."

"Good night, Sam," she says, backing away and then turning to walk quickly across the dew-damp grass, up the steps to the porch and around the house. A minute later, I hear her car start, back up and pull away, the sound of the engine fading into the night.

My head begins to pound in its usual spot, and I stand, staring out at the lake until the pain reaches a new threshold, something in its intensity feeling almost deserved.

A promise is a comfort for a fool.

~ Proverb

Gabby

I can't sleep, but it's not as if I expected to.

My head is filled with a collage of images that cut back and forth between this new Sam and the boy I remember.

The new one is a man — with all the subtle nuances that go along with life experience and the hard knocks required to obtain it. It has changed the way his eyes see the world, and there's a wariness to him that I never knew before.

Before.

Before we made plans to spend our life together. Before he left here when we were teenagers. Before he married another girl. Before my heart got shattered into too many pieces to ever fit together exactly right again.

I'm aware that at my age this sounds melodramatic and overstated.

But when you're seventeen and the boy you love moves out of the country with his family, there really aren't any words to describe that kind of pain.

The night he told me that his family was moving out of the country, I truly thought I would die. We were on a date, what I'd thought to be a normal one, except for the fact that he was quieter than usual. No joking. No smiles. It was July, and we'd gone out on his parents' boat, found a cove to skinny dip in, and then lay on the bow staring up at the stars.

He'd reached for my hand, his grip tight. Without taking his eyes from the sky, he said, "I have something awful to tell you, Gabby."

My heart knocked once and then set up a rapid rhythm. "What?" I asked, suddenly scared that something was wrong with him.

"My dad—he's been transferred to South Africa."

I heard the words, and, yet at first, they made no impact. They just sat on the surface of my understanding, like raindrops on wood. "What do you mean?" I asked, even as I realized how stupid the question sounded.

"He told me this afternoon. He and Mom say Ben will stay here because he's already in college, but that I have to go with them and do my senior year of high school there."

I'd never really thought about what it would feel like to be punched in the stomach with the full force of a strong fist. But that was the only thing I could think to compare it to, a feeling of having had all the oxygen knocked from my body.

Sam rose on one elbow, cupped his hand to my face. "I can't stand it," he said. "The thought of being without you for that long—"

A sob erupted from my throat then, the sound harsh and pain-filled. Sam leaned down and kissed me hard, as if he could think of nothing else to do to ease the anguish in us both.

I slipped my arms around his neck and kissed him back with a desperation I had never before felt. As if I could feel him slipping from my grasp with each passing second. And all I wanted was to hold him to me so that nothing could ever take him away.

Before that night, we had never actually made love. We'd been as close as we could be without crossing that line, both of us wanting to wait until we were married. We believed it was right, and that what we felt for each other was worthy of it.

But in those moments of frantic fear, I could think of nothing but wanting to be as close to him as it was possible to be. Still naked from our swim, the temptation was too great to resist, and with only the slightest prompting from me, Sam let me know that it was what he wanted too.

Maybe the nature of loving someone is that you don't realize what you have until you are faced with losing it. We both knew that night. I had never before and have never since been consumed with that kind of love, wishing that I could literally melt into him, be a part of him that could never be left behind, as I was surely going to be.

Making love with him was everything I'd imagined it would be, except for the sadness I felt afterward, lying in his arms, wishing for some way to make the night last forever, wishing we could run away.

As if he'd read my mind, Sam had said exactly that. "We could leave," he said. "Go somewhere where our parents couldn't find us. Start our life together now."

I'd felt myself caving to the possibility, pure grief for all that we were facing screaming at me to do so. But I'd thought of my dad, the heart attack he'd had a year ago, my mom and the pain it would cause them. I wanted to scream at the unfairness of it. How could anything this cruel happen to us? "It would kill them," I said. "Your parents and mine."

"I know," he said, his voice breaking on the words. "But a year. What if you meet someone else? What if you—"

I stopped him then with a kiss that made no secret of the fact that there would never be anyone who could replace him. "Don't," I said. "You know how I feel about you."

He ran his hand up my bare leg, let it settle

possessively on my breast. "I love you, Gabby. I love you so much."

"I know. I know you do."

Looking back, I guess that was when we had surrendered to what was ahead for us. I believed with all my heart that we would survive that year, that he would come back to me, and we would pick up where we left off. That nothing or no one could permanently separate us.

One year was what we would have to suffer through until Sam turned eighteen. I couldn't imagine how, but we were determined to focus on that point in our future, even though it seemed like a hundred years away.

We made plans for when he could legally make the decision to return here without his parents. We both wanted to go to the University of Virginia, and we would get married so that we could live together there.

And of course we would write and talk on the phone as often as we could.

This was our survival plan, and we were six months into it when I got the letter from Sam.

The letter that ended it all. The letter that made me realize none of it, not a single moment of it, had ever been the least bit real.

Yesterday is gone. Tomorrow has
not yet come. We have only today. Let us begin.
~ Mother Teresa

sam

My headache is gone when I wake up just after sunrise. I feel energy coil inside me and decide to go for a run even as I question the wisdom of it. But I refuse to let the worry unravel. I've never lived my life like that, and I'm not going to start now.

The morning air of spring is still crisp and fresh, and I run the country roads with an appreciation for the beauty around me that I can't deny I'm seeing with new eyes. For so many years, I've lived on a sort of autopilot. Plowing through my days at the hospital as if there were an unidentified finish line to be crossed somewhere ahead in the future.

In doing so, I've missed a lot.

Color, for example. It's as if I'm now aware of it as I've never been before. The green of the mountain on my left. The blue of the lake I catch glimpses of here and there.

Maybe I got used to the frequent rainy days in London, and things just seem brighter here, more vivid. But I don't think that's it. It's more like I've spent my adult life in a place that was not my home, and I could never see it as such.

And this place, this place I once loved as my own, has continued to call me back.

I think about Gabby now—realize I've been putting it off—and let myself remember what it felt like to sit beside her last night, nearly shoulder to shoulder. How familiar it was to be with her that way, just sitting by the water and talking, even though it has been twenty-five years since we last did so.

I run to the end of the state road where a high-rise condominium is poised at the end of the point. The view from here is the best on the lake. I stop and take in the wide expanse of water, watch the early morning fishermen speeding to their favorite coves. I wait for my breathing to slow and then head back the way I came, my pace slower now, not from a lack of energy, but so that I can process the feelings knocking around inside me.

In coming here, I don't think I let myself consider that I might still have feelings for Gabby. Too many years had passed, too much pain had been endured and shelved to ever consider revisiting any of it.

But the door between the past and present is a thin one, and I can already feel its give. I wonder how it can possibly hold back the inevitable.

I spend the rest of the morning keeping myself busy with repair work to the house. I fix a few shutters that are hanging crooked, sand down the porch steps and make a note to buy some paint when I go into town.

I'm at the top of a ladder cleaning out a gutter when I remember David Lanning, a guy I went to med school with in London. I'd heard some years ago that he was practicing at Duke in North Carolina, and a mutual friend had mentioned that he'd become a pediatric surgeon with a specialty in bone diseases.

Next to my brother, David had been one of the smartest guys I'd ever met, and he had the kind of devotion to learning that made him a professor favorite.

I get down off the ladder and retrieve my cell phone from the house, coming back outside to sit on the steps and Google the main number at Duke. An operator there connects me to David's office, and a receptionist tells me that he is in surgery. I leave a message with my name and number, and only then do I consider the fact that I have probably grossly overstepped my bounds in making the call. But I've already left the message, so I get back to my busywork, keeping the phone in my shirt pocket in case it rings. Which it does, just after two o'clock.

"Sam," David says. "Is that really you?"

"Yeah. It's been a lot of years, huh?"

"Too many to count. How are you, man?"

"Good," I say. "And you?"

"Can't complain. Few aches and pains here and there, but who doesn't have them? Are you still in London?"

"Until recently," I say. "I'm actually in Virginia. Smith Mountain Lake?"

"Yeah, beautiful place. What brings you there?"

"My folks had a summer place here when I was growing up. I'm visiting for a while."

"Well, you're just a couple hours down the road from me. It'd be great to see you."

"I'd like that." I hesitate, and then, "I was actually calling for your professional opinion on something, David."

"Shoot."

"A friend of mine has a daughter with osteogenesis imperfecta."

"I'm sorry to hear that," David says.

"She has a deteriorated disc that keeps her in pain, especially when she stands or walks. Because of it, she spends a lot of time in a wheelchair."

"How can I help?"

"I don't know if you can, but her mother has seen numerous surgeons who consider her case high-risk."

"Would you like me to take a look?" David asks.

"That would be a huge favor."

"For an old friend? Not at all."

"Thanks, David. Should I have my friend call your office to schedule the appointment?"

"Yes, that would be fine. Will you be coming with them?"

I haven't thought of this, and my answer reflects it. "I'm not—I don't know for sure."

"Well, I hope so. It'd be really great to see you."

"You too. Can't thank you enough."

"Okay, then. Take care, Sam."

"You too, David."

I click off the phone and sit down on my newly sanded steps. Now all I have to do is tell Gabby what I've done.

It is kindness to immediately refuse what you intend to deny.

~ Pubillius Syrus

Gabby

I'm in the cafe totaling up register receipts when the phone rings. I pick up the old-fashioned handset, answering with the standard "Hayden's Marina." Hearing Sam's voice, I'm caught off guard and pretty much stutter a hello.

"How's it going?" he says.

"Pretty good," I say, with a hint of question in my reply.

"I was wondering if you and Kat might be up for a picnic on my boat tomorrow."

I hesitate, and then say, "Sam. Do you really think that's a good idea?"

"I don't know. Maybe not. But I do have something important to tell you."

Unable to imagine what it could be, I wonder at the

serious note in his voice. "What time were you thinking?"

"Noon?"

"Okay. Noon it is," I say.

"Great. I'll see you then."

He hangs up, and I place the receiver back in its cradle, wondering what it is he could possibly have to tell me.

"Um-hmm."

I look up to find Myrtle studying me with a knowing grin on her face. "Um-hmm, what?" I say.

"Um-hmm you're talking to that fella who liked my grits and collards."

"You never forget a fan, do you?" I say with a reluctant smile.

"No, ma'am. So when are you going to tell me the real story about him?"

"There is no story," I say.

She gives me one of her familiar harrumphs. "There's a story."

I feign intense concentration on the calculator and my batch of receipts, but she's still waiting when I look up. "We knew each other when we were kids."

"Old friend, huh?"

I can tell she's buying that, like she'd buy full-price Christmas paper on December twenty-sixth. "It was a long time ago."

She walks into the kitchen, picks up a dish towel and

starts wiping down the countertops. "Didn't look to me like either one of you had forgotten much of anything," she says.

"That's not a place I'm going."

"Been my experience that we don't always get to choose where the heart takes us."

I'd like to argue with her, but I can't seem to find any words that feel like they'd be convincing enough.

"Did I hear you say something about a picnic tomorrow?"

"It's not that kind of picnic."

And we're back to, "Uh-hmm."

Kat rolls through the door just then, glancing back and forth between us both. "What picnic?" she asks.

"The one you and your mama are going on with that handsome Mr. Tatum tomorrow."

I throw her a look. "Just how much of my conversation did you listen in on, Myrtle?"

"Enough," she says, chuckling.

I'd like to be mad at her, but no one can be mad at Myrtle for long, including me. "Sam called to see if we'd like to go out on his boat tomorrow," I say to Kat.

"Cool," she says. "He seems nice."

"Don't he, though?" Myrtle says with a little kick in her voice.

Kat looks from one of us to the other. "Did I miss something?"

"No," I say quickly. "Did you finish up your schoolwork?"

"I did," she says, keeping her gaze on me.

"Why don't we go to town for a pizza?" I say, eager to divert the conversation.

"Or we could see that new movie and have popcorn for dinner instead."

"Child, what kind of dinner is that?"

Kat laughs. "A good one."

Myrtle looks at me and shakes her head.

"I know," I say. "I'm a total pushover."

"When it comes to her, you are," she says.

I kiss Kat on the top of her head. "Popcorn and a movie it is."

The first recipe for happiness is: avoid too lengthy meditation on the past.

~ Andre Maurois

Sam

The night is a restless one in which I sleep in fits and starts, finally giving up altogether around four o'clock. Downstairs, I make coffee and read a few cardiology journals I've been meaning to get to for a while. Articles I'd once read to help me maintain my edge as a sought-after physician.

I'm halfway through the second one when it occurs to me that I might not ever get the chance to use whatever knowledge I gain here. That maybe it's just a waste of time to add another speck of information to what I know.

It's not as if I haven't thought it before. But here, in this place where I was once so full of life and hope for the future, I grab hold of the anger that flashes through me like lightning and make myself finish the article before closing the journal and putting it away. I get dressed and head out for the local minute market, determined to focus on the day ahead and nothing beyond that.

I'm the first customer, rolling my cart down the aisles and looking for items I think either Gabby or Kat will like. I end up with enough food to feed a dozen people. I put a few things back, so I'm left with what looks like a more reasonable offering, big red Florida-grown tomatoes, a fresh-baked loaf of bread, and mayo to make up the main meal. I haven't eaten tomato sandwiches in too many years to count and remember them as a staple of summer lunches here when I was a boy. I add a bag of Fritos and cans of Grape Crush to the cart, aware that I'm not going to win any nutrition points from Gabby for my efforts.

I head back home with my purchases and put the lunch together way too early, so that I'm left with nothing to do but think about the journal I'd been reading earlier, and the feeling of futility about whether there was even a point to it. I begin to wonder then if I am wrong to interfere in Gabby's life. To start something I might not be able to finish.

Short of calling her and canceling, there is nothing to do but follow through. I lower the boat from its slip around 11:30 and motor towards the marina at a speed that allows me to pull in just short of noon.

Kat is waiting on the dock, waving when she spots me. "Hello," she calls out.

"Ahoy there," I call back.

She smiles as if I'm the corniest man she's ever met. "Mama's coming in a minute."

"How are you?" I ask, sidling up to the dock and jumping off, tying the ropes at the front and back.

"Good. Pretty day for a picnic," she says.

"It absolutely is," I agree.

Just then, Gabby comes out of the cafe, Myrtle behind her with a basket. They both call out hello to me and then Myrtle adds, "Made you all a pie for your lunch. Strawberry."

"That sounds amazing," I say. "Thank you, Myrtle."

"I'm just glad to see you getting these two out of here for a bit, so they can do something other than work."

"Myrtle—" Gabby begins.

"Well, it's the stone-cold truth. Been trying to get you to take a day off since Lincoln was shot."

Gabby shakes her head and gives Myrtle a look with which I suspect the older woman is well familiar.

"Can I leave my chair here, Mama?" Kat asks Gabby.

"Sure, honey. If you think the boat seats won't hurt your back."

"I'll be fine," she says, a stoic note in her voice.

"Okay," Gabby says, and then glancing at me, "Ready?"

"Yep," I say, taking the basket from Myrtle and giving it an appreciative once-over.

"Now y'all just take the afternoon and relax. Timmy and I have got this place covered."

"We will," Kat says, and I can see Gabby's getting ready to argue, but Myrtle waves and hurries back inside.

A few minutes later, we're cruising up the cove and away from the marina. Kat is propped on the cushioned back seat and has popped in earbuds for her iPhone. I avoid any waves and drive slow enough not to bounce for fear of causing her pain.

I risk a sideways glance at Gabby in jean shorts and a T-shirt, both of which she wore with the same appeal when she was seventeen. She catches me looking, and I jerk my gaze away.

"Any particular place you two like to go?" I ask.

Gabby points toward the mountain. "Anywhere along there is nice."

I aim the boat in that direction, and we motor over in an awkward kind of silence. When we get closer, Kat pulls out an earbud and says, "Are we going to swim?"

"The water's still cool," Gabby says, looking at me with a smile of chagrin.

"I like it that way."

"We'll see after we eat."

And then Kat's back to her music.

"What is it you wanted to talk to me about?" Gabby asks, the breeze slightly lifting her hair so my eyes are drawn to the curve of her neck.

I glance away, focusing on Kat who is swaying to a tune we can't hear. "I hope I haven't overstepped my boundaries, but I made a call to an old friend of mine. David Lanning. He's a pediatric surgeon at Duke who specializes in bone diseases. We went to school together in London."

Gabby's gaze is fully on me, her eyes wide with surprise. When she says nothing, I go on, faster now, maybe a little afraid she'll cut me off. "He's agreed to see Kat and review her case, if you would like for him to."

Gabby's look is one of utter surprise, and it's clear this is not what she expected at all. "I can't believe you did that."

"I know I should have asked you first—"

"No. I mean, thank you." Tears spring to her eyes, and she turns her face into the wind, blinking hard. And then she looks at me again, "Why would you?"

"I'd like to help," I say. "That's all."

She says nothing for a stretch of silence, and since I don't know what she's thinking, I remain quiet, too.

"It's been so hard," she says, "hearing over and over again how she'll just have to live with this."

"David might agree," I say, not wanting to get her hopes up.

When she looks back at me, I see the gratitude in her eyes, and I think I understand for the first time the weight of the responsibility she has been carrying.

"Thank you," she says again. "I don't know what else to say."

"Nothing is needed," I tell her, and our gazes lock and hold for a moment, before I force mine back to the water ahead.

We pick a spot at the base of the mountain where a strip of sand allows us to beach the boat. I help Kat out and set up three folding chairs at the edge of the water. She walks along the edge for a minute or two and then sits, a hand at the base of her spine.

"Is the pain constant?" I ask Gabby as we carry the picnic food to the blankets we've spread out on a grassy spot.

"If she's standing, it's nearly constant," Gabby says.

And I can only imagine how hard it would be at Kat's age to know you couldn't run and play like other children. "She doesn't question it, though, does she?" I say, setting down the basket.

Gabby shakes her head. "I've never known anyone so determined to make the best of what they have. But that's Kat."

"Do you think that comes from her early childhood?"

"Maybe. At some point, she decided she was okay with the hand she got dealt, that she would make the best of it, I guess. She wants to be a doctor—she says she thinks she'll be able to help her patients because she can understand how they feel."

"And I believe she will."

"I do think she was shaped by some of what happened to her before her life here. Not that she remembers much of it. But she has an appreciation for the simple stuff that goes beyond what I see in most children."

We empty the basket, spreading out the food on one of the blankets. I move a fold-up chair over closer for Kat, and she pulls out her earbuds, thanks me and sits down.

"This looks awesome," she says, glancing at the tomato sandwiches.

"I think Myrtle might have topped my menu with that pie."

"May I say the blessing?" Kat asks, and we bow our heads to her simple thanks for the food and the day.

I'm surprised by her initiative, and I think how many years it has been since I heard my own children pray.

We take our time eating, and I think we could not have ordered a more picture-perfect afternoon.

"May I use the float for a little bit?" Kat asks once she's done, pointing at the one I'd thrown in the back of the boat.

"If it's okay with your mom."

"As long as you wear a lifejacket."

Kat and I head for the boat where I hand her the jacket and pull out the float. She climbs on, flat on her back and paddles outs, earbuds in place.

"Thanks," Gabby says, when I sit back down on the quilt.

"No problem."

"You've been a good father, haven't you?"

The question surprises me, but I try to answer honestly. "Not perfect by any means. I probably should have worked less when they were young, but I did try to make time for doing the things they liked to do. I'm afraid they were a bit spoiled. Analise, my daughter, is in the throes of teenage rebellion."

"That must be hard."

"It's sort of like you have to batten the hatches and wait for the storm to pass."

"And it will," she says.

"I just hope soon enough," I say. The thought is out before I can censor it, and Gabby looks at me, curious.

"What do you mean?" she says.

I struggle with a response, but finally add, "Before she forgets she once loved me, I guess."

"She won't," Gabby says, convincingly. "In fact, her love for you will probably be even stronger."

"I would like to think it's true. But it's hard. We were once so close. I could do no wrong. Now I can do no right."

"It's the cruelest phase of parenting, I think," she says. "They have to pull away to become independent. It would be nice though if the bandage didn't have to be ripped off."

"That's pretty much what it feels like."

"I can't imagine Kat reaching that point. But I know

that she will. I did. As much as I loved my parents, we had a few rough spots."

"That's hard to believe. You were so close to them."

"I was. But after you left—" She stops there.

"After I left, what?"

She doesn't answer for a bit, and when she does, she looks at me directly. "I went a little wild, I guess."

I try not to think about what exactly that could mean. "I'm sorry, Gabby."

"For which part?" she asks, meeting my gaze.

"All of it."

"Me too," she says.

Regret surrounds us like suddenly descending gray clouds. "Gabby," I say softly, "if I could change—"

"You can't," she interrupts with an edge to her voice. "We can't."

"I know," I concede.

I glance out at the float where Kat is lying face to the sun, one foot dancing in time to her silent music.

"At one point in my life," Gabby says softly, "I would have given anything to reverse the clock, go back and have a chance to live the life we thought we would live. But now, I can't wish for any of it to be different because if it had been, I wouldn't have her. And you wouldn't have your children."

"Kind of hard to know how to think about it," I say.

"It is," she says, tracing a finger in the sand. She

makes a tic-tac toe board, puts an X in the top left corner.

I write an O in another spot, and in silence, we play out the game we used to play on summer days on the sandy beach next to my parents' dock. Gabby wins, drawing a line through her row of Xs.

I place my hand on top of hers, my heart jolting in remembered connection. We sit like that for several long moments, and then she turns her hand so that our palms are facing. Our fingers link together, and we hold on tight. I close my eyes and absorb her touch, instantly realizing that I've lived my life convinced that what we once felt for each other couldn't possibly still exist. Only now I realize it's just been dormant, never actually extinguished, but simply waiting for the right conditions to reignite.

Happiness floods through me, just this wash of pure emotion that I haven't felt in so long. But right behind it is guilt. I don't have the right to reopen any of this with Gabby. I've already hurt her once. I can't do that again.

I remove my hand from hers, aware of her questioning gaze even as I do. We sit for several moments, not saying anything, me unwilling to meet her eyes, because I'm afraid of what I'll give away.

She's the one to finally speak first, her voice neutral of any physical awareness. "Are your parents still living?"

"No," I say, shaking my head. "My dad was killed in a car wreck about ten years ago. My mom died of a stroke two years later."

"I'm sorry," she says. "I should have asked you sooner."

"It's okay."

"I'm sorry you lost them so close together."

"She was miserable without him. To be honest, I'm surprised she lived as long as she did after he died."

"It's pretty great when people love each other like that, though."

We're on awkward ground again, and I can't look at her because I can't hide the fact that this is the kind of love I felt for her. "It is," I say, keeping my gaze on the water where Kat is floating in what appears to be utter contentment.

"Why are you here, Sam?"

The question is out of nowhere, and I find myself without an automatic response. "It's complicated," I say.

"I already guessed that." She keeps her gaze on Kat, still floating and waving her arms to music only she can hear.

"Why would you come back after all this time?"

"I needed to," I say, and this is true. "Loose ends, I guess."

"With me?"

"That's one part of it."

"Surely you know it's way too late to fix any of that." The response is a little harsh and edged with hurt.

"I don't expect to fix it. I just want you to know I'm sorry."

She pulls her knees to her chest, wraps her arms around her legs, as if she's trying to keep herself together. "This doesn't make any sense, Sam. I don't want to dig it all up again. I made peace with us a long time ago."

"I'm not asking you to."

She looks at me then, and I see a storm of confusion in her eyes. "Maybe we should head back," she says.

"Gabby," I say, putting my hand on her arm.

She stands and calls loudly across the water to Kat.

Kat pulls off her headset and rises on one elbow.

"It's time to go," Gabby says.

Kat looks disappointed, but paddles in. "Anything wrong?" she asks, looking at us both.

"We just need to get back," Gabby says, her voice now neutral.

"Aww," Kat says. "It's so nice here."

Gabby starts gathering the picnic things, and we reload the boat in silence. And the entire time, I am asking myself what had made me ever think we could get past the past.

Life is really simple, but we insist on making it complicated.

~ **Confucius**

Gabby

It feels as if we'll never get back to the marina.

The air between Sam and me is now heavy with awkwardness. I don't know what to say to him, and he doesn't know what to say to me.

Sam pulls the boat up alongside the dock, and I start to gather our things, when Kat lets out a startled cry.

I drop the quilts in my arms and run to her. "What's wrong? Are you okay, honey?"

She's white as snow, and her gaze is on something beyond the cafe. I look up and spot her wheelchair hanging from the limb of the old oak tree that stands just up the hill. I feel as if someone has pushed all the air from my lungs. I instantly pull Kat to me, my heart breaking when she starts to cry.

Sam has now seen it too, and he quickly finishes tying up the boat, then jogs to the tree and untangles the chair from the bungee cords holding it up. He lowers it to the ground and rolls it back to the dock.

But Kat wants nothing to do with it. She thanks Sam for getting it down in a polite voice and disappears into the cafe.

"Who would do that?" Sam asks, looking at me with anger in his eyes.

I sigh heavily and run my hand through my hair. "Probably a couple of boys who live down the road. I don't know why, but they've made Kat the target of their pranks. A while back, they put a frog in her purse at church. Before that, they left a black snake in the mailbox."

Sam frowns. "How old are they?"

"Thirteen."

"Sounds like they're getting more brazen."

I nod, the worry nagging inside me inching up a notch. "At first, it seemed pretty harmless. But now," I say, glancing at Kat's rescued wheelchair.

"You mind if I get in on this?"

"Sam, you don't have to do that."

"I want to."

"And do what?"

He smiles a half-smile. "I was a boy once. All right if I borrow Kat for a couple hours in the morning?"

"She's usually finishing up her schoolwork around eleven."

"Eleven is good." He steps onto the boat, then turns

to look at me. "I'm sorry for the way the picnic ended. I shouldn't have gone into—"

I feel petty, like a person carrying a grudge that suddenly looks overplayed. Maybe it is. Maybe it isn't. I can't seem to tell anymore. My emotions are in a jumble, and I can't make sense of what's going on inside me.

"I'm the one who's sorry," I say. "You were unbelievably kind to make that call to your friend about Kat."

"You don't need to apologize for anything."

The sun is strong on my shoulders, and I meet Sam's intent gaze with a near feeling of lightheadedness. The protective part of me is poised in flight mode, but another part, the part that once loved him beyond what I have words to describe, caves ever so slightly. And I am intensely aware of his dark hair, his strong shoulders, the awareness in his eyes.

I can't say for sure what it is, his kindness toward Kat, his quiet, reassuring strength, or the physical chemistry that is still so readily identifiable between us.

Maybe it's all three. But in those moments, standing outside under a spring sun, I feel the love start to return.

~

ONCE SAM LEAVES, Kat goes to the house, and I help Myrtle finish cleaning up in the cafe kitchen. She is beside herself when I tell her about the wheelchair hanging in the tree.

"Why didn't I hear those two hoodlums out there doing that? And why aren't those boys in school today?"

"I don't know," I say.

"Sneaky little devils," she says. "They better hope I don't catch them when they're up to no good. I'm not too old to swing a frying pan."

I smile a little at the image of Myrtle chasing them down the road with her cast iron skillet. "Kat tries to act like it doesn't get to her," I say, "but I know it does."

"And why wouldn't it?" Myrtle is all but shaking with anger. "Somebody needs to kick those boys' butts."

"Sam's cooking up some kind of payback."

Myrtle nearly drops the soup pot she's been drying. "Oh, he is, is he?"

There's teasing in her voice, but something else, too, that says it's about time somebody started looking out for Kat and me. "Don't go making something big of it, Myrtle," I say.

"Nice-looking man like that actin' on your behalf. I'd say that's somethin'."

"That's what friends do," I say.

"Is it now?" She puts the pot on the counter, shakes out her drying cloth. "Um-hmm."

And we're back to that again.

~

AFTER DINNER, Kat and I watch a movie on Netflix. I make a big bowl of popcorn, and we sit on the couch with the lights off, because we like for it to feel as much like we're at the movie theater as possible.

This is one of her favorites, *Hachi: A Dog's Tale*, a story about a dog so devoted to his owner that he waits for him at the train station every day, even years after the man dies. We've seen it three times before, but I cry with the same abandon this time as I did the first. Kat cries too, and we sit there, arms wrapped around each other, while the credits roll by.

"Why do we do this to ourselves?" I ask her.

She sniffs and wipes the back of her hand across her face. "Some things are worth the tears," she says.

"How old are you?" I tease, pulling back to look at her.

"Ten," she says.

"Oh, yeah." I hug her to me again and tell her then about Sam's plan to pick her up in the morning.

"To do what?" she asks.

"I think he has a little plan in mind for the Smith boys."

She smiles now. "Really?"

Her enthusiasm surprises me somehow, but then I guess this is not something she's known before, a man in her life willing to go to her defense. "You okay with that?"

"Better than okay."

We clean up the dishes and head to bed. I tuck her in, kissing her good-night with a poignant awareness of her excitement for the outing with Sam. I'm glad, but I'm also wary of her becoming attached to him, when I know he's not here to stay.

I put on some music and sit down at my desk to pay bills. I'm not sleepy; my brain feels like it's on overload with all the questions circling around inside it.

The computer on my desk is like an open box of cookies, tempting, beckoning. I put away my checkbook and hit the space bar. The screen lights up. I click on the browser and pull up Google.

When the box appears, I type in Sam's name, along with a few other identifying factors. London, England. Cardiologist.

Believe it or not, I've never done this. I've thought about it, but then left it alone, one of those doors I knew I was better off not opening.

A glut of references pops up. I click on the one at the top that lists Sam as a partner in a London cardiology group. The website cites him as one of three doctors. There is a photo of him—looking very serious and distinguished—unlike the man in shorts with whom I'd just spent the afternoon. A short bio describes his practice and his belief in the importance of a patient taking control of his or her health with lifestyle changes and choices.

I read every word like they're drops of water, and

I've been in the desert without. I click back and link to another site where I find pictures of him with a woman I presume to be his wife. The caption below reads:

Dr. Sam Tatum and his wife, Megan, donors to the Bonham cardiac wing of Mercy Hospital in London.

She's pretty.

I can't deny it.

No, she's beautiful. Like one of those supermodels who've reached forty without a single worry line. I can't even see evidence of Botox assistance. Her skin is smooth and unlined. Her dark hair long and straight. In the picture, she's wearing a short black dress that shows lengthy legs.

Next to her, Sam is dressed in a tuxedo, and he looks ridiculously good in it. They are a stunning couple, and an objective part of me thinks what a shame it is that they are no longer together. Like a beautiful pair of bookends separated and no longer functional.

But then I notice that neither one of them is smiling—and I wonder how I missed that. They're not touching either, standing side by side, poised as if they'd been caught off guard in being asked to pose for the shot. I glance at the date of the photo. Two years ago.

They'd been miserable. It's clear to see. I wonder for how long.

Strangely, I don't feel any gladness for this

realization. Some part of me had always thought that Sam would be happy in his life without me. And maybe deep down, I'd felt some comfort in that.

It feels like a crazy admission, considering our history, but I wonder then, if that might be the real definition of love. Caring about someone else's happiness even when it doesn't include you.

~

SAM CALLS BEFORE I've had my first cup of coffee.

"Morning," he says.

"Morning," I say. "You're up early."

"Have you seen the Moon?"

"No."

"Take a look. It's still out."

I walk to the window and pull back the curtain. The sky has started to lighten, but the Moon hangs like a giant beach ball, translucent yellow with clear markings throughout. "It's beautiful."

"My room was so bright when I woke up; I thought it had to be daylight."

I remember that about him—how his mother had said when he was a little boy, he'd wake at the first ray of light in his room, how she'd tried dark curtains and window shades, but even the slightest speck of light brought him wide awake. I feel a morsel of tenderness for the memory and the fact that in this, he is still the same.

In all fairness, I realize that in many ways, he's still the same.

There's a heaviness to the silence between us, as if there are things we both want to say, but don't know how. I don't mind it though. It's nice just knowing he's on the other end.

"Gabby—"

I rush to stop him, hearing in the tone of just my name that he's going to say something I'm not ready to hear. What's happening between us feels fragile and vulnerable, and I want to protect it from too much too soon.

"You'll be here at eleven, right?" I rush in.

"Eleven."

"Okay. We'll see you then."

He's quiet for a moment, and then, "Enjoy the Moon," he says and hangs up.

The duty of comedy is to correct men by amusing them.

~ Moliere

sam

I get to the marina a few minutes early, and Kat is already waiting for me. She's rolling her chair back and forth in the driveway, looking nervous.

"Hey," I say, getting out.

"Hi," she says, smiling, her blue eyes lighting up.

Gabby comes out of the cafe then, a dishtowel in her hands. She's wearing jean shorts, a white tank top and flipflops. Her blonde hair is loose and shines in the sunlight.

"All right if I have her back in a couple hours?"

"Okay," she says. "Should I say have fun or be careful?"

I smile, and our gazes hold for a moment. "We won't wreak too much havoc."

"As long as I don't have to bail you out of jail," she says.

"We'll keep it short of that."

Gabby gives Kat a kiss on the cheek. I put her chair in the back of the car, and she gets up front with me. We back out of the drive and pull away, Gabby still watching from the front yard.

"So what are we doing?" Kat asks, with barely restrained curiosity.

"First, we'll need the boys' phone numbers," I say.

"Okay," she says carefully. "They have cell phones."

"Can you get the numbers for me?"

"Sure," she says and taps the screen on her phone.

She chats a couple of minutes with a girl named Sarah who's apparently also homeschooled – I hadn't thought about that – and then pulls a paper from her purse and writes two numbers on it. The girl apparently asks why she wants them because Kat says, "I'll tell you later, okay?"

She hangs up and looks at me. "Got them. What's next?"

"Next is the local newspaper office."

She smiles. "And what are we doing there?"

"We're gonna see a man about an ad."

And her smile grows bigger.

~

AT THE NEWSPAPER OFFICE in Rocky Mount, we both go inside and I write up the ad:

Premium cow manure needed for scientific

experiment. Please contact Lance Smith or Tom Smith at either number listed below. Need is immediate. Call anytime, night or day.

Kat reads over it and giggles.

"When will this be listed?" I ask the young woman behind the front desk.

She glances at the clock on the wall behind her. "It should make tomorrow's edition."

"Great," I say. "How much do we owe you?"

We get back in the car, and Kat says, "Where to now?"

"Now, we'll go see a man about some cow manure."

She laughs. "You're really good at this."

"Nichols Dairy, here we come."

I'd made some calls to local dairy farms first thing this morning and found one that had what we would need. It is only about ten miles away, and we drive the county roads with Kat pointing out sights along the way. Tonk's Country Store. The elementary school where she would go if she weren't doing homeschooling. Her best friend Sarah's house.

I like hearing her talk. Her voice is soft with its southern inflection, and it's uncanny how much she sounds like Gabby. Not just in word choice, but with a particular lilt to certain words.

"You and my mom used to be friends?" she asks in a surprise change of subject. "When you were young?"

I hesitate, debating what to say, but then realize the truth is the only version I can tell. “We were.”

“She acts funny around you. She doesn’t normally act that way. Around men, I mean.”

“What way?” I ask.

“Like she’s nervous and doesn’t want to say the wrong thing.”

“I probably act the same way around her.”

“You do,” she says, matter-of-factly. “You liked each other as more than friends?”

I take a deep breath and wonder if I’ve taken on more than I bargained for. “We did.”

“Do you still now?”

“I don’t really know how to answer that, Kat. I’ll always feel something special for your mom. But we’ve lived separate lives for a lot of years.”

“I thought people stayed together if they loved each other. Why didn’t you?”

“It’s kind of complicated.”

“Mama said you moved away.”

“I did. But not because I wanted to.”

“Why didn’t you come back?”

“I kind of messed all that up,” I say.

She gives me a long, assessing look, as if she’s trying to decide how much of a bad guy I am when it comes to her mom. “You mean with another girl?”

“Ah, yes. With another girl.”

“I bet that hurt my mama.”

"It did," I admit, realizing Kat is not your typical ten year old. "It's one of my biggest life regrets."

"And we don't get re-dos, do we?"

"No. Not very often, anyway."

"She must have really missed you when you left."

"I missed her too."

"There it is!" she says, pointing ahead to the Nichols Dairy farm turn off, and I'm off the hot seat, at least for now.

I swing a right and follow the gravel road to its end where a two-story white farmhouse stands to the right. Out to the left is the barn operation, black-and-white cows milling about as if they're waiting to be let in for the next milking.

I stop just short of the barn, and a young man in coveralls and a John Deere hat strolls out to meet us. He smiles big when he sees Kat, then glances at me as if questioning why we're together.

I get out and walk around, while Kat rolls down her window and calls out, "Hey, Hank!"

"Hey there, Kitty Kat! Whatcha doin' out here?"

"Mr. Tatum brought me."

"Sam," I say, sticking out my hand to Hank.

"Howdy do," he says, nodding once.

"I'm a friend of Gabby's. Kat and I are out on a little errand today."

"What can I do for you?" he asks.

"I called earlier about buying some cow manure."

"Well, we got plenty of that," he says, laughing.

"We just need a couple buckets full," I say. "I talked to someone who said that would be all right."

"Sure thing. You plantin' a flower bed or somethin'?"

"Not exactly."

He looks at me with clear curiosity as we grab the buckets from the back of the Explorer. Kat says she'll wait in the vehicle, and I tell her we'll be right back.

To the side of the barn, he grabs a shovel, and we walk over to a trailer that's hitched to a tractor. "We spread this on the fields," he says. "Best fertilizer there is."

"I guess so," I say.

We fill up the buckets and carry them to the Explorer, setting them in the back. "What do I owe you?" I ask.

"Not a thing," he says. "Come back anytime."

I thank him, and we pull away, Kat waving out the window.

~

WE DRIVE TO THE top of the driveway, where each of the boys will get off the bus later in the afternoon.

Kat giggles nonstop as I carry the buckets to their spot and jog back.

Once I'm in the vehicle, I look at her and say, "Mission accomplished."

She offers me a high-five. "Mission accomplished."

"Dairy Queen to celebrate?"

"Awesome," she says. She looks out the window and then in a more serious voice, "Thank you, Dr. Tatum."

We lock eyes for a moment, and I can see what it means to her that she's had someone go to bat for her. "Sam is good with me. And you're more than welcome," I say.

Real kindness seeks no return; What return can the world make to rain clouds?

~ Tiruvalluvar

Gabby

While Sam is out with Kat, I call Dr. Lanning's office and speak to the receptionist. I explain that a friend of mine, Sam Tatum, had spoken to Dr. Lanning about an appointment. She is immediately aware of the referral and says that Dr. Lanning had told her to expect my call.

I'd been nervous for some reason, worrying that I would have to explain my connection to Sam or why he had called for me. I realize how ridiculous that was when the receptionist transfers me to a nurse who had also been told to expect my call. Her voice is soft and southern, and she asks me a series of general medical questions about Kat, which I answer with practiced ease.

"Would next Monday at nine o'clock work for you to see Dr. Lanning?" she asks.

"Ah, yes," I say, not expecting him to see her this quickly.

"He had a cancellation and asked me to hold it for you."

"That's very kind," I say, realizing the breadth of the favor Sam has done for us.

"All right then," the nurse says. "I think we have everything we need for now. We'll see you next week."

"Thank you so much," I say and hang up.

I stare out the window of my small office. Two ducks glide gracefully across the lake, side by side. I've been alone for so long that I hardly know what to do with the feelings battling inside me — resistance to letting anyone else help me for fear that when I'm alone again — I won't be able to shoulder the responsibility as I have done. That maybe like a muscle, my ability to do everything I can for Kat will atrophy if I'm not using it full force.

Even as the thought races through my mind, I know it is ridiculous. Sam has simply connected us with a doctor he thinks might be able to help Kat. There's nothing more to it than that.

But then honesty tugs at my conscience, and I have to admit that my reservations are nothing more than my own fear of getting hurt again. Hurt as I have only been hurt once in my life. By Sam.

A car rolls into the driveway. I pop up from my chair and go to the front door. Sam and Kat are back. She's in the front seat, smiling and then laughing at something Sam has said. I watch them, amazed at how natural it seems to see them together, and how only a week ago I could not have imagined opening our lives to him in even the smallest way.

But that is exactly what I'm doing. I feel the pull of it from a force far stronger than I will ever be. Resistance is my flight response. But my heart is directing differently. I just don't know if I'm strong enough to listen.

Sam gets Kat's wheelchair out of the back and she sits down in it. He rolls her to the house.

"Mama!" Kat calls out.

Only then do I step away from the window and open the front door. "Should I even ask what you two have been up to?"

Kat laughs and says, "It was so great!"

I smile at her exuberance and then look at Sam, noticing now that his face is pinched, as if he's in pain. "Are you okay?" I ask.

"Yeah," he says, brightening a little. "Just a headache."

"Can I get you something? I have some—"

"Thanks, but I have something at the house. I should be going." He backs up and steps out into the grass. "You're a good partner, Kat," he says.

"You too," she throws back.

"Okay. I'll see you then."

He strides across the grass and gets in the car, but not before I see the look on his face, and a new worry sets up inside me.

~

KAT IS IN GOOD spirits the rest of the afternoon. When I ask her what they had done, she says, "Can it be a secret just a while longer?"

"Was it anything dangerous?" I ask, hearing how silly I sound.

"Mama. Of course not."

"Okay, then," I concede.

And she's all smiles again.

We hang around the house the rest of the day, doing normal things: I work on the website I've been setting up for the marina, Kat reads a book that is part of her homeschool curriculum. And all the while I can't quit thinking about Sam. About the look on his face just before he left this afternoon.

After dinner, I ask Kat if she would mind if Myrtle came over for a bit. She looks at me, clearly curious, but says, "Nope."

I call Myrtle and ask her if she can stay with Kat for a couple of hours, and to my surprise, she doesn't ask me where I'm going. But then I suspect she knows and is probably doing a high-five on the other end of the phone.

I take a quick shower and change into jeans and a

pink V-neck T-shirt. I blow dry my hair, spritz on my favorite perfume and concede to a little lipstick.

When I walk into the living room, Myrtle has arrived. She and Kat both glance up from the checkerboard they are playing on and look at me, wide-eyed.

"My goodness," Myrtle says.

"You look pretty, Mama," Kat adds.

"Thanks," I say.

"Are you going to see Sam?" she asks in a voice that makes it clear she already knows the answer.

Myrtle smiles and says, "Goin' to see somebody important."

"Don't make something of it that it's not," I chastise them both.

"We're just goin' by the clues," Myrtle says, giving me a once-over. "And you do look pretty."

I kiss Kat and leave the house with warm cheeks, embarrassed by my own transparency.

Nothing makes us so lonely as our secrets.

~ Paul Tournier

Gabby

The drive to Sam's doesn't seem nearly long enough. I pull into his driveway with my stomach in knots. I should have called first. I can't just show up out of the blue. But I am worried about him, and I tell myself that's the only reason I'm here. Well, the main one, anyway.

I knock at the back door and then wait a minute before rapping again. His car is in the drive so he must be here.

I start to knock again when the door opens, and Sam stands before me, his eyes groggy.

"Hi," I say, awkward now and wondering what in the world I had been thinking to just show up like this.

"Hey." He runs a hand through his hair, looking self-conscious.

"Are you okay?" I ask.

"Yeah," he says, nodding. "I took something. It makes me kind of out of it."

"Migraine?" I ask.

He nods once, and says, "Come in."

"You're probably better off going back to sleep," I say.

"I'd rather not," he says, and I can hear in his voice that he's glad I'm here.

I walk in the door, and then follow him to the kitchen. He flips on the light and blinks once, rubbing his eyes.

"Have you had dinner?" I ask.

"No. I've actually been asleep since I got back from your place."

I'm a little surprised, but cover it up with, "Can I make you something?"

"You don't have to do that, Gabby."

"I'd like to," I say. "I'm not as good a cook as my daughter or Myrtle, but it will be edible."

"That would be great. Do you mind if I take a quick shower?"

"No," I answer quickly, "go ahead."

"Be back in a few minutes. Make yourself at home."

"Okay." I watch him disappear and listen while he walks upstairs. I remember his old room and the times we had made out there when his parents were out of the house. We had been so young, learning about love together, neither of us more experienced than the other. My lips tingle in remembrance of the first time Sam ever kissed me, and I touch my fingers to them, then blink away the memory and check the refrigerator for something to cook.

Eggs, a Vidalia onion and some feta cheese. That should do. I pull out a frying pan and put everything together for an omelette. I throw a couple pieces of bread in the toaster on the countertop, and the kitchen is soon filled with the smell of cooking.

Sam is back just as I finish up the omelet and slide it onto a plate.

"Wow. That looks so good," he says.

"Thanks." I put the plate on the table, and he sits down.

"Are you eating too?" he asks.

"I had dinner earlier," I say. "You go ahead."

He digs in with enthusiasm, and I feel suddenly glad to be here. Why, I can't exactly put my finger on. I just know it feels right for now.

When he finishes, I put my hand on his arm. "May I ask you something?"

His face becomes instantly guarded, but he nods.

"Is everything okay with you, Sam?" I ask, and there's worry in my voice.

Something in his eyes goes soft. "I'm all right," he says.

I hold his gaze for a moment, looking for something more, even though I'm not sure what. Relief spills through me, and I can't explain my concern. Maybe it's simply that what has happened in the past week is beyond my own imaginings — that Sam would ever come back here — that anything of what we once felt for each other might actually still exist.

But sitting here next to him, I am unable to resist this fluttering of desire and hope entwined inside me. And so I believe him. What reason do I have not to?

Life is a sum of all your choices.

~ Albert Camus

Sam

It feels utterly strange at first, sitting in the kitchen of my childhood with Gabby, both of us adults with a long stretch of years we've lived with little to no knowledge of each other.

I eat the food she has prepared, each bite tasting better than the previous one, and I wonder about the man who had been her husband, what kind of life they had together.

"How long were you married, Gabby?" I ask, the question out before I can think better of it.

She looks up at me, surprise widening her eyes and then says, "Eight years."

"Where did you meet?"

"At UVA. My junior year."

I feel a rush of irrational jealousy for the fact that she had met someone there, the college we planned to attend together. The fact that we hadn't was my fault and mine alone, and I guess some of this must show on my face because she gets up from the table and puts the frying pan in the sink. She starts to scrub it with a sponge, her back to me, her shoulders stiff.

"What was he like?" I ask, forcing neutrality into the question.

She doesn't answer for a few moments, and then, "One of the nicest people I've ever met."

Her answer catches me off guard. I'd expected something more typical of divorce, a note of bitterness, at least. But there was none. Only regret. "Oh," I say. "What—why did you—"

She turns from the sink then and stares directly at me, her arms folded across her chest. "Do you want complete honesty?"

I nod once, not at all certain that I do.

"He wasn't you, Sam," she says, her voice raspy. "That was his only fault. No one ever has been you."

The pain in her expression is like a blade in my stomach, and I slide back my chair, stand with my arms aching from the need to pull her to me. I don't give myself time to think about it. I go to her and reel her in.

She is unyielding at first, her body rigid against me. I press my lips to the top of her hair, then my cheek to her forehead. She instantly goes soft, a sound of submission breaking from her lips.

"I'm sorry," I say. "I'm so sorry." And I'm not even

sure what I'm apologizing for. One thing. Or a thousand things.

I hold her face in my hands, and we stare at each other for a string of seconds. In her eyes, I read all the pain she's felt over what I did, and something inside me collapses with grief and sorrow. "Gabby—"

But she stops me before I can finish, pulling my face to hers and pressing her lips to mine. The kiss is at once shocking in its unexpectedness, and yet so utterly familiar. We're both tentative at first, testing, tasting, and then I deepen the kiss, and it's exactly as I remembered, sweet and right in the way of something lost and again found.

I think that I could kiss her for the rest of my life, just like this, and nothing more. I run my hands down her long hair; anchor them at the small of her back. She drops her head and makes a sound that I remember, one of longing, of surrender.

We come apart as if in a dreamlike trance, pulling back to look at each other with something like disbelief, as if neither of us can believe we're really here. That this is really happening. "I've had this exact dream so many times," I say, brushing the back of my hand across her cheek. "But every time, I woke up to realize that's all it was. That's all it would ever be."

"And that was your choice," she says, and her voice has anger at the edges. "It didn't have to be like that, Sam. I loved you."

"I loved you," I say.

She pulls away and crosses the room in an obvious need to put distance between us. "How can I believe that?" she asks, anchoring a hand on the countertop, her knuckles whitening.

I want to tell her everything. I need to tell her. My hesitation is not for fear that she will hate me more once I do, but that I will hurt her more in doing so. And yet, I know I have to.

I sit down at the table again and ask her to do the same.

She does so reluctantly, pulling her chair back so that we're farther apart, like she needs that space to be objective.

"I never meant for any of it to happen," I say, and already I'm wincing at the lameness of my start. She waits for me to go on, her expression now blank. "I missed you so much, Gabby, I actually thought I might die from it."

A flicker of emotion crosses her face, and I can see that it's what she felt, too.

"One night, I went out with some guys I met at my school. They'd been trying to get me to go with them for weeks, and I never wanted to. I don't really know why I went that night, except that you and I had talked the day before, and I could hear the distance growing between us, like our lives were being filled up with other things and other people to the point that pretty soon, there wouldn't be room for each other. Or at least that's what it felt like then."

"And that's the night you met her?" she asks, the question breaking a little at the end.

"We'd gone out drinking at this place where girls from a nearby private school hung out. I had way more than I should have, and by the time she and I started dancing, I was nearly stumbling drunk. I don't even know how we ended up back at her room. And I don't remember having sex with her."

Gabby slides her chair back and stands, a sound coming from her throat, as if someone has knocked the breath from her. "I don't think I want to hear anymore," she says.

"There's no excuse for what I did, Gabby," I say. "And I'm not trying to make one. I just want you to know the whole truth."

"That you had sex with another girl!" she cries then, "when you were still telling me how much you loved me?"

"And that was true."

"So what? You fell in love with her after one night together? One night when we'd planned to spend the rest of our lives together?"

I look down at my hands, then force the words up from where they've been buried inside me. "I never fell in love with her."

"You married her!"

"She was pregnant."

Gabby's gaze snaps to my face, shock widening her eyes. "From that one night?" And then shaking her head, "That certainly sounded stupid."

"I didn't know until a couple of months later. I didn't see her again after that night until the day she came to tell me."

She turns to the sink, bracing one hand on either side and dropping her head forward. I push back my chair and cross the floor to place a hand on her back. She whirls around as if my touch has burned her.

"What is it that you want me to take from this, Sam?" The question is ragged and torn from her, like tape from a wound.

"I just want you to know that I know I messed up in the biggest possible way."

"That you cheated on me in a one-night stand and got a girl pregnant? What am I supposed to say? Oh, that's okay. Now I understand everything."

"I don't expect you to say anything. I just needed you to know—"

"What? Know what?"

"That I never meant to hurt you. That I screwed up. That hurting you the way I did—I've never been more sorry for anything in my life. And if I could—"

"Change it?" she finishes.

I start to say yes, and then I find that I can't because

I see my son's face and then my daughter's, and I can't say something that would deny their existence.

It's as if she's read my mind because all the fight goes out of her, like a windsock that has lost the breeze.

"How can we look back from here and question any of it?" she asks.

"I can't," I say. "I love my children."

"And I love my daughter."

It's beyond difficult to stand in front of the only woman I've ever loved, in the way I think true love was meant to be, and say these things. What I want is to erase every single moment of pain I ever caused her, but I can't. I will never be able to do that.

She looks at me now, confusion clouding her eyes. "I think I should go," she says.

"Gabby, please, wait—"

"I did that for longer than you would believe," she says. "Don't try to stop me, Sam. I'd like to say I have the ability to resist you. That anything I ever felt for you is just part of the past, but I think you know that's not true. Please don't take advantage of that. Just let me go."

The selfish part of me wants to do exactly that. Take advantage of a moment when vulnerability might trump common sense. But I don't. I simply stand here and watch her walk out of the house, listen as her car starts and then backs out of the drive.

The house is suddenly too quiet.

I've never felt this alone.

A true friend is one soul in two bodies.

~ Aristotle

Gabby

I have no idea where to go or what to do. I just know I can't go home right now.

I call Myrtle and ask if she can stay a while longer. She says of course she can, and she must hear something of what I'm feeling in my voice because she doesn't even tease me about what I'm likely to be doing staying out so late.

I drive without any destination in mind, taking turns simply because they are there, until I suddenly find myself on the road to Annie's house.

The driveway to the Winston farm is long and winding, rutted in spots and lined with four-board fencing on either side. In the dark, my headlights glance off the shadows of cows grazing in the pastures.

The old brick house sits at the end of the drive. It was built in the late 1800s. I've always loved it, as much for its quaint southern welcome as for the large, loving family that lives here. It's Annie through and through, big Sunday get-togethers, summer cookouts and a vegetable garden big enough to feed her entire neighborhood through the winter.

My best friend since elementary school, Annie has the life I'd once imagined I would have with Sam. She'd married Scott Winston, a boy she met in high school around the same time I met Sam. They have five children, who all look exactly like a blend of them both, tow-headed like Scott, green-eyed like Annie.

It's nearly eleven now, and I know Scott, who sleeps farmer's hours, has long been in bed. Annie's a night owl like me, and I won't be waking her up.

Just as I turn off the engine, the door opens, and she steps out on the front porch, squinting and then waving as she recognizes my car. She tiptoes out in doggie-emblazoned pajamas and bare feet, stopping at my lowered window.

"Hey," she says, concern wrinkling her small forehead. "What are you doing out so late?"

"Can we talk?" I ask, just before tears roll up and spill down my cheeks like someone has turned on a waterfall inside me.

Annie opens my door, and I step into her outstretched arms. She hugs me hard against her, and all I can think is that it's been a really long time since anyone comforted me this way. I sob for a good minute or more, unable to stop myself, even as I realize how ridiculous I must look.

Annie rubs my back and says it's okay, then takes my arm and leads me to the front porch, where we sit side by side on a wooden swing. The porch is half in shadow, and we swing back and forth, arms entwined.

"Gabs, what is it?" Annie says.

"You're not going to believe it."

"Try me."

I try to find the words, and then just blurt out, "It's Sam—he's staying at his parents' house."

"Sam Tatum?" she asks, incredulous.

I nod, not meeting her gaze.

"Have you seen him?"

"A few times, yes."

"Wow." She releases a breath. "Do you think that's a good idea, Gabby?"

"No."

She sighs and rubs a hand across my hair. "Hey, I was here for the original fallout, remember? I'm not sure your heart can handle another letdown from him."

"We're not—I mean, nothing is—"

"Gabby. If the two of you are anywhere near each other, it's going to be something."

I'd like to deny the accusation, but I can't. So I don't bother. "He came to the marina a week or so ago. It was such a surprise that I pretty much lost it with him."

"And?"

"He said he deserved it."

"I guess that's good to know. Have you seen him since?"

I nod, wipe the back of my hand across my wet cheek. "Kat and I went on a picnic with him. He called a pediatric surgeon friend of his who's going to see her on Monday at Duke."

I glance out at the dark pasture just beyond the house, make out the shapes of a few dozing cows.

Annie can't hide her worry. "Are you sure you want to do this to yourself, Gabby?"

"I don't know. At first, I didn't want to see him. I just wanted him to leave again."

"Why is he here?"

"I'm not really sure. He and his wife divorced about a year ago."

"Did he come back here for you?"

"No," I say, adamant. Even if there were any truth to the possibility, I'm too scared to believe it.

I drop my head back against the top of the swing and sigh. "I went over to his house tonight."

"Mistake number one."

"He kissed me."

"Mistake number two."

"I wanted him to."

"That's number three."

"I'm just so furious at him!" I cry out.

"For kissing you?"

"No! He told me something tonight that I have no idea what to do with."

"Unless it was I'm-sorry-Gabby-but-I-got-knocked-on-the-head-twenty-some-years-ago-and-have-been-comatose-since, I don't see what he could possibly say that would justify what he did to you!"

I try to hold onto it, but I feel the heat of my anger disintegrate like ash beneath a wind. My voice is small and a little broken when I say, "He slept with a girl one time and—"

"She got pregnant?" Annie asks, incredulous.

I nod once.

"And this changes what?"

"Nothing. I don't know. If you could have heard him—"

"You are NOT going to fall for this sob story, are you?"

"I'm not falling for anything, Annie. I just—"

"You're falling for him all over again, aren't you?"

"No, I—"

"The truth is you never fell out of love with him."

I start to deny it, but there's no point. I'm not going to convince either myself or Annie. Annie who knew me when I was trying to put myself back together all those years ago.

"What does he want from you, Gabby? A fling that he can take back to England as a memory? You're really not going to serve your heart up on that platter, are you?"

"I can't," I say.

"No, you can't. Do that to yourself, I mean. Maybe you've forgotten what it did to you before when he left, but I haven't."

"I haven't forgotten."

"Then don't do that to yourself again."

I try to dredge up at least a piece of my former anger, the anger that Annie is feeling, but I can't find it now in the numbness crowding my chest. "I don't know how to think about this."

"Gabby! He cheated on you with another girl. He got her pregnant. He married her. Maybe they didn't live happily ever after, but he made a life with her, not you!"

The words hurt. I can't hide it. And they're out there, raw and wounding.

Annie grabs my hand and clasps it in hers. "I'm sorry, Gabby. That sounded so awful."

"It's true, though."

Annie chooses silence over agreement, and we sit, swinging for a good bit before I say, "If he hadn't done that, if we hadn't broken up, I wouldn't have Kat."

Annie tips her head, starts to say something, stops, and then says, "And you're going to let that condone what he did?"

"No. But don't you ever wonder why things happen? Why we don't always get what we want, when we want it? That maybe God has another plan in store for us that can't happen if we're the ones making the choices?"

"I don't think God wanted Sam to cheat on you, if that's what you're saying."

"Maybe it's just that we don't always understand why things happen when they do. It's only later that we can see what would or wouldn't have happened."

"You're playing an unfair card," Annie says.

And maybe I am. Because I do know that Annie has questioned such things in her own life. Like the accident Scott had been in five years ago and the fact that she and the girls had nearly gone with him at the last minute. The vehicle he'd been driving had been completely demolished in every single spot except for the driver's seat and the left front end. Before that, Annie hadn't been to church since her girlhood, but she'd gone on the Sunday following the accident, and she hasn't missed one yet, to my knowledge.

"If it applied to you, why shouldn't it apply to me?"

"Scott didn't mean to get into a wreck!" Annie protests.

"I'm not sure Sam meant to do what he did, either."

She gives me a "you've-got-to-be-kidding" look. "This is one wreck I can clearly see is going to happen," Annie says, her voice resigned. "You're about to have a head-on crash, Gabby."

It's been a long time since we've had anything close to an argument. Most of our conversations these days revolve around raising children, how to stay fit and which vitamins are really worth taking. We haven't touched on romance in years. Mostly because I haven't had one, and somewhere along the way, I think Annie started feeling guilty for being so happy in that department.

"I have no intention of doing anything stupid, Annie. I'm just trying to make sense of it."

"I love you, Gabs. I don't want to see you hurt again."

"I know," I say. And it's true. She's as close to a sister as anyone has ever been to me, and we look out for each other in that way. But sometimes I don't think she understands what I felt for Sam. "It's the same as what you feel for Scott, Annie."

"What?"

"The way I feel—felt about Sam."

She starts to disagree, then seems to think better of it.

"I know you don't believe that, because if it had been the same, it would have lasted."

"I don't think—" She stops and then shakes her head. "Well, maybe I do think that. Because wouldn't it have lasted?"

"I don't believe he thought I could ever forgive him."

"Would you? If you had known?"

I want to answer with an immediate yes, but I guess I don't really know whether I would have or not. The me considering the question in the here and now is a very different me from the seventeen-year old I had been then. "I don't know."

"I'm being hard on you, aren't I?" Annie says, tipping her head against mine.

"Maybe a little."

"But when he leaves—as he surely will—"

"I know."

We sit for a while, swinging back and forth, the night around us silent, except for the squeaking of the swing's chains.

"So, what are you going to do?" Annie asks after a bit.

I don't answer for a moment, but it's not because I don't know what I'm going to say. There's only one thing that makes any sense at all. "Nothing. I'm going home."

I stand and walk to the top step of the porch before turning to say, "I'm sorry for bringing this to you."

"Gabby, I'm here for you," she says, guilt lacing the words. "Always."

"I know," I say.

"I want you to be happy."

"I am. I was. Before Sam came back. And I will be after he leaves."

"I feel like I've given you a really bad scolding."

I try to smile, but the edges of my mouth don't seem to be working. "I guess I needed it."

"Call me," Annie says as I get in the car.

I pull away, sure that she is no happier at having delivered her opinion about what is best for me than

I am to receive it. But then bitter medicine is never pleasant to dispense or to take.

Not life, but good life, is to be chiefly valued.

~ Socrates

Sam

My ringing cell phone pulls me from a groggy sleep. I raise up on an elbow, squint a look at the clock beside the bed. 5:30. I glance at the cell. Analise. A quick mental calculation. It's 10:30 a.m. in London.

I fumble for the phone, knock it on the floor and then quickly pick it up. "Hey, honey."

"Daddy. Hi. The ring sounded funny on your phone."

"Oh?"

"Like it does when you're in another country or something," she says.

"Actually, I am."

"What?"

"In another country. The states. At my parents' old lake house."

There's a moment of shocked silence, and then, "When did you go?"

"A few days ago," I say. "Last week, really."

"Why—did anyone know you were going?" she asks, and I can hear the hurt in the question. As if I might have told everyone but her.

"No, sweetie. It was a last-minute thing."

"But I don't understand why you didn't tell us you were going."

"I was going to call—"

"When?" she says, sounding more like the parent now than the child.

"Analise, I knew you were busy with school, it being close to the end of the year and—"

"Not too busy to take a phone call from you," she protests.

I want to remind her that isn't exactly true. There have been plenty of times when she's asked to call me right back and never did. But I don't say any of that, simply, "I'm sorry, honey."

"What are you doing there, anyway?"

"I just needed to get away for a little while."

She sighs as if she can't imagine this is true, after all what would I have to get away from, and then, "Well, how long are you going to be gone?"

The question is directed with all the outrage of offended youth. "I'm not exactly sure."

"How can you not be sure? What about your practice and your patients?"

"I've taken a hiatus of sorts."

"Daddy!?! What is going on?"

"It's just something I need to do right now," I say.

"Are you having a midlife crisis?" she asks, her tone indicating her certainty that this can be the only possible explanation for my irrational behavior.

It sounds so silly and flimsy to my ears in comparison to the reality, that I wish it were something that insignificant. "No. It's nothing like that."

"Then what is it?" she insists.

"I just needed to get away," I say, and this is true.

"I could have come with you," she starts, and then, "School is nearly out you know."

"I know, but I kind of wanted to come now."

"Oh," she says, sullen like a seven year old. "Well, I wish you'd waited."

I'm sure I was every bit as unreasonable to my parents, and so I simply apologize again.

"What are you doing there all by yourself, anyway?"

"Revisiting old places, old friends."

"I didn't know you still knew anyone there."

"A few people."

"Does Mom know you're there?"

"No," I say, and try my best not to remind her Megan no longer has any right to know where I am. I'm not exactly sure why, but even though Megan had been the one to bring about the demise of our marriage, Analise seems to see me as the culprit.

"Are you going to visit Uncle Ben?"

"Yes, in a week or so."

She's quiet and then, "I really do wish I were there with you, Daddy."

My heart melts a little at the words. It's been a long time since Analise has sounded this way—like a girl who misses her daddy. The past couple of years have been hard on us both, her transition from my little girl to teenager and then figuring out how to have a relationship with me that does not include her mother. "I would love to show you this place. I'm sorry I've never brought you."

"Me too. It feels like a part of you we've never known."

It is a soberingly accurate statement. And I guess I have to admit I have kept this part of my life from them. Whether it was to protect them or protect what I'd had here, I don't know that I can say for sure. "I'm sorry, sweetie. I'd like to right that sometime."

"When are you coming back?"

"I'm not sure yet."

"Before I get out of school in two weeks?"

"Maybe not," I say, only now realizing I have mentally extended my stay.

"May I come there then?"

"If I'm still here, yes."

"Okay," she says, and there's relief in her voice, as if this at least makes sense to her. "Does Evan know you're there?"

"No, but I'll call him today."

"It's really strange, Daddy, that you would go without telling us. Promise you won't do that again?"

"I promise. I love you."

She hangs up without responding. I lie in bed for a good while after we hang up, trying to sort through what I'm feeling. Guilt for coming here without telling my children. And the undeniable reality that I can't hide out here forever.

We never know the love of a parent till we become parents ourselves.

~ Henry Ward Beecher

Analise

I will never be a parent.

To be a parent, you have to be utterly selfish and have the ability not to care a bit how you affect the lives of your children. To be able to get a divorce and go on as if you were never a family of four, and all your history can just be obliterated with the signing of a document.

I should know. I ended up with two perfect examples of this.

I stare at my phone screen, debating whether to call Mom or not. I hear students talking outside my dorm room, laughing and rough-housing, as if their lives are just perfect. I have to resist the temptation to open the door and yell at them to shut up.

I finally give in and call her. She answers out of breath.

"What are you doing?" I ask.

"Yoga. Hold on just a minute, honey."

I sit on my bed, tapping out the seconds until she returns with, "Sorry, just grabbing a towel. How are you?"

"Have you talked to Dad?"

She hesitates as if I've thrown her a trick question. "No, Analise. I haven't. We're not really talking these days."

"So I guess you didn't know that he went to the states?"

"What?" she asks with enough surprise that I'm happy I've thrown her a curve.

"He's at that lake where he used to go with Grandma and Grandpa."

"I had no idea."

"Obviously."

"Analise," she says, an irritated note in her voice. "Could you please try to work your way toward cutting your father and me the slightest bit of slack?"

"I called to see if you had a guess as to why he went without telling us," I say, ignoring her request.

"I have no idea, Analise. Maybe he needed a vacation."

"He usually tells us things like that."

"Maybe he has a girlfriend."

"That doesn't bother you in the least, does it?"

"We *are* divorced, Analise."

"Must be nice to have a license not to care, Mom," I say and hang up.

I try to call Evan, but get his voice mail. I send him a text.

Do you EVER answer your phone?

I sit on the bed for a while longer, waiting for him to respond, but that ends up being a waste of time.

I think about the list of friends I have here — not a very long one — and scroll my contacts for Helen Dintry. Unlike my brother, she answers on the first ring.

"Hey, girl," I say.

"Analise," she says, my name lilting up at the end, as if she can't believe I'm calling. "Thought I was on your no-ring list."

"I've just been trying to keep up with the studying."

"Down with that. You're not going to ask me to be your study buddy, are you?"

I laugh a little. "No. Anything going on tonight?"

"There's a lot going on, actually."

"Good. I feel like getting trashed."

Now she's the one who laughs. "Well, you certainly called the right girl, didn't you?"

Life appears to me too short to be spent in
nursing animosity or registering wrongs.
~ **Charlotte Brontë,** ***Jane Eyre***

Sam

I spend the morning with my dad's old toolbox and a ladder, providing first aid to some of the house's less notable needs, a drooping gutter, a stuck window and bowed flooring. I let the work blank my mind of last night with Gabby, this morning's conversation with Analise.

The effort is less than successful because it's Gabby I'm thinking about when the phone rings just before lunch.

It's Kat with bubbles in her voice. "Guess what, Sam?"

"What?"

"Sarah, my best friend, has a cousin who rides the school bus with Lance and Tom. She said they got three calls each this morning on the way to school from people about the cow poo ad."

"Really?" I say, smiling.

"Yep. She said their faces turned beet red, and they finally just turned their phones off." She laughs, and there's sunshine in the sound.

"We did good then?"

"We did good." She hesitates and then, "Thank you, Sam. For helping me."

"You're more than welcome."

"I never would have come up with anything like that."

"That's a good thing, I'm sure."

She laughs. "Can I fix you supper tonight? As a thank you."

I'm debating what Gabby would say about that when Kat says, "Mama says it's okay."

"You sure about that?"

"Positive."

"Maybe I ought to talk to her first."

"Okay," she says, and I can hear her curiosity. "Mama?" she calls out.

There's some rustling of the phone, and then Kat says, "Here she is."

"Hey," Gabby says.

"Hi. It's fine if you'd rather I not come. I didn't want to put you in an awkward position."

"Kat wants you to."

I start to argue, but the part of me that wants to go doesn't want to give her a chance to change her mind. "Okay, then. What time?"

"Be here at six?"

"Six, it is."

"See you then," she says and hangs up.

~

I GET THERE FIVE MINUTES early and debate sitting in the driveway until I'm on time, but Kat looks out the front window of the house and comes rolling out the door to meet me.

I get out of the car, and she's in front of me in seconds, her face lit with a smile. "Sam! They're asking everyone if they know who put that ad in the paper. No one does, and I'm the last person they'd ever guess would do it."

"That's a good thing," I say.

"I guess. Even though I'd sure like to see the look on their faces when they found out." She turns back to the house, rolling along beside me as I walk to the front porch. I give her a push up the ramp, and Gabby meets us at the door.

We study each other for a moment, everything I'd practiced on the way over so much wasted effort since my mind can't get a foothold on a word or a thought. "Thanks for having me," I finally say, and it feels as lame as it sounds.

"Come in."

I follow them both through the living room and into the kitchen where something smells wonderful. "Um," I say. "What is that?"

"Kat is doing homemade pasta tonight," Gabby says, by way of explanation.

"It's a surprise past that," Kat says. "You and Mama are banned to the deck while I finish."

"Honey, I planned on helping," Gabby says, as if she's just spotted a pothole ahead that she hadn't anticipated.

"But I want to do the whole thing," Kat says, and I see Gabby waiver between her desire to avoid being alone with me and her recognition of her daughter's sincerity. "I already put iced tea and glasses out there for you, so shoo."

We're left with little option but to do as she says, and Gabby leads the way through the sliding glass doors, shutting it behind us.

"Sorry about that," I say.

"She wants to repay you," Gabby says. "I understand."

"She doesn't owe me anything."

"That's not how she sees it." Gabby picks up the pitcher of tea and pours us both a glass.

"Thanks," I say, taking it and immediately setting my gaze on the lake beyond the deck when what I really want is to linger on Gabby's face and the troubled look in her eyes.

"Do you think, for tonight, because it's important to Kat, that we could just forget about everything we talked about last night?"

"Yes," I say, wanting to add that I'd be happy if we could permanently erase all of it from both our minds.

The sliding glass door opens, and we both turn to see a woman holding a plate with a very large cake that has been decorated in pink swirls of icing. She glances at Gabby and then at me, her eyes widening.

"Oh," she says. "I didn't know you had company."

I recognize her then as Gabby's friend, Annie. She's actually changed very little in all the years since I've seen her, her dark hair still straight and long, her blue eyes wary of me. "Hello, Annie," I say, standing.

"Ah, Sam. Hi." She looks at Gabby and says again, making a point, "I didn't know you had company."

"Kat's making dinner," she starts to explain, and then as if thinking better of the explanation, "Would you like to join us?"

Annie holds the cake up and says, "Just wanted to drop off a peace offering."

"You didn't have to do that," Gabby says.

"Maybe it wasn't needed." Annie shrugs, and sets the cake on a nearby table.

Feeling the tension, I say, "If you two would like to talk, I can go inside."

Annie holds up a hand and shakes her head. "No, no, I think everything has already been said."

"Annie," Gabby starts, but Annie slides open the door and disappears into the kitchen.

"Aren't you going to go after her?" I ask.

Gabby is standing with her back to me, facing the lake. "It's probably not a good time."

"Would you like for me to go, Gabby? I'm sure Kat would understand if you told her—"

She turns then, her eyes snapping fire. "Told her what? That we used to love each other and being anywhere near you now is like having a knife stuck in my heart?"

It isn't what I expected, and, judging from the look on her face, I don't think it's what she meant to say either. But she doesn't take it back. She leans forward with her hands anchored on the deck railing and draws in a deep breath.

"It would have been better," Gabby says, "if you'd never come back at all."

"In a lot of ways, I think you're right."

"In every way that counts."

"Gabby—"

She whirls around, cutting me off. "I went to her house last night after I left yours. She thinks I'm crazy to have anything to do with you."

"She may be right about that."

"She cares about me, Sam, and doesn't want to see me hurt again."

"And I don't want to hurt you."

"You are, though."

I have a sudden feeling of panic, like I'm at the top of

a roller coaster about to head down the other side when it stops, poised to torpedo off the tracks.

I set my glass of tea on the table next to the cake. "I'll tell Kat I can't stay. I shouldn't have come. I knew you were doing this for her, and I guess I took advantage of it."

My hand is on the door when she says, "No. Don't. She's worked hard this afternoon."

"Are you sure, Gabby?"

"Yes," she begins, just as Kat opens the door and announces that dinner is ready and waves us inside with a big smile of anticipation.

"I'll leave as soon as we're done," I say to Gabby once Kat has planted us both at the dining room table and disappeared into the kitchen.

"Okay," she says, and it's clear to me that I have at least, for now, said the right thing.

I felt it shelter to speak to you.

~ Emily Dickinson

Gabby

Kat likes him. A lot. On some level, maybe it should bother me, but, for some reason, it doesn't. It's easy to see why she does, after all. He listens when she talks, not like some adults who listen at half attention, but with real interest in her opinion.

She's telling him about a book she just read, *Fever 1793*, set in Philadelphia during the yellow-fever epidemic that wiped out 10 percent of the city's population. "You're a doctor. Can you imagine living through such a thing?" she asks, directing the question to both of us.

"No," Sam says. "People literally died overnight, didn't they?"

Kat nods. "The girl who's the main character in the story lost her mother. It was so sad," she says and looks at me with such love that I am instantly reminded how lucky I am to have her as my daughter.

Sam sees it too, and I wonder about that flash of longing on his face, whether he's missing his children. "It would be horrible, wouldn't it?" he says.

Kat nods. "Do you have children?"

I flinch at the question. It's innocent of anything other than curiosity, and she has no way of knowing the awkwardness of it.

"Yes," Sam says. "Two."

"What are their names?"

"Evan and Analise."

"Are they my age?"

"They're older than you," Sam says, and I find myself waiting for him to elaborate. But he doesn't.

"Do they like to read?" Kat asks.

"My son does. He started reading when he was three. There was just something about words that he loved."

"Me too," Kat says. "I even like to read cookbooks."

Sam smiles. "Lucky for us."

"You like it?" she asks, nodding at the food on his plate.

"I love it. What is it?"

Kat laughs. "Pansotti alla genovese."

"Ah. That's what I was thinking."

He looks at me, and I smile without editing myself.

"It's Mama's favorite," Kat says.

"That it is," I agree.

"How did you start cooking?" Sam asks, glancing at Kat.

"To help Mama. She hates to cook."

"Which has worked out great for me," I say.

"And me," she agrees.

"What is it you like about cooking?" Sam asks.

She thinks about the question for a moment, and then says, "Foods are like an artist's paints. The colors are beautiful, but they taste good too. You can make something pretty and appealing, and it makes people happy."

"Hard to beat that," he says.

"I like to make people feel good. That's why I want to be a doctor."

"That's an awfully good reason to choose a career."

"Do you like being a doctor?"

"Yes."

"What kind are you?"

"A heart doctor."

"A cardiologist."

Sam smiles. "Yes. That one."

"I'm sure it makes people happy when you fix them."

"You're right. It does."

Kat spears a ravioli with her fork, as if thinking about whether to say what she's about to say. "Can a heart really break, Sam? I mean like for real."

Sam's gaze widens, and then he looks at me.

Something near my own heart lurches, and I tear my gaze from his.

"Sort of, yes," he says.

"I know the veins get stopped up and stuff sometimes. But I mean like from love. Can a heart break from that?"

"I think it hurts in a way that a person can feel it."

"Is it something you can fix?"

"Most of the time it's the kind of thing that can only be fixed by the person who broke it."

I can't listen any longer. The blood is pumping through my veins with alarming intensity, and I can feel the pulse beating at my temple. I get up from the table, say, "Excuse me," and swing through the door to the kitchen.

There, I plant a palm on either side of the sink, and draw in several deep breaths. The heat has started to leave my face when I hear the door swing in and feel Sam's presence behind me.

"Are you all right?" he asks quietly.

I turn around and force neutrality into my smile. "Yes. I'm fine."

"I'm sorry about that—"

"She doesn't know," I say.

"Yes, but I could have derailed that conversation."

"Why didn't you then?" I ask, wondering at the note in his voice.

"Because I think it's true."

"That you broke my heart?" I try to sound disbelieving, but hear my own failure.

"That I broke both our hearts."

It's not what I expected, and the only response I can find is, "Sam."

"Mama!" Kat calls out. "Aren't you and Sam going to finish your food?"

"We're coming," I call back, and leave Sam standing there with undeniable regret etched in his face.

~

THE REST OF THE MEAL passes with Kat doing most of the talking, this time avoiding anything as serious as hearts. She plants us both on the deck and serves dessert out there, leaving us to finish and talk while she cleans up the kitchen.

By now her efforts at matchmaking are fairly transparent, and I wait for the door to close behind her before looking at Sam and saying, "I'm sorry."

"You don't need to apologize to me. I'm just glad she thinks I'm worthy of you. Coming from her that would be a high honor."

"Sam—"

"I can leave if you'd like."

"No, stay," I say, realizing how much I do not want him to leave. "Your children. Are they like you?" I ask.

He looks surprised by the question, but says, "Some parts are. Evan likes learning new things, taking stuff apart and figuring out how to put it back together again."

"Like hearts?"

"Yeah," he says, smiling. "Only that's not going to be his choice of puzzle. He's studying law."

I nod. "And Analise?"

"She might be a writer. She's been keeping journals since she was seven. She's pretty much written down every thought or feeling she's had since then. She's developed a strong, unique voice. And when she's a little older, I think she's really going to have something to say."

"They sound a lot like you."

"They're good kids. We've had our moments. Analise is currently living the rebellion phase, but hopefully, it won't last."

"How do you know?" I ask, suddenly picturing Kat pulling away from me, unable to imagine the pain of that.

"I guess you just have to trust that if they've loved you once, they'll return to that. That's the cruel part of parenting, the fact that you have to let them go, in order for them to ever come back."

"And the harder you hold on, the more they pull away?"

"Something like that, yeah."

"It sounds awful."

Sam smiles. "It kind of is while you're in the middle

of it, but once it passes, you don't really remember the pain of it."

"Like childbirth. Or so they say."

Sam takes a sip of his coffee, and I can see he's weighing his next words. "Did you ever try to have a child?"

I shake my head. "No."

He clearly wants to ask more, but doesn't. "She couldn't be any more like you if she were your natural-born child."

"Thank you," I say. "It's nice to hear that."

"It's true. She even has the same facial expressions as you."

"Really?" I ask.

"Like the way you squint your nose when you don't agree with something."

"She does do that."

"And the way you twist your finger through your hair when you're thinking hard about something."

I laugh now, picturing Kat doing exactly that, and realizing I'd never recognized it as something we both do. It's nice, though, to think that Sam noticed.

The sliding door behind us opens, and Kat says, "Was it good?"

"Scale of 1 to 10?" Sam asks.

Kat nods.

"Fifteen," he says.

Her smile is instant. "Cool. There's more if you'd like it."

"Thanks, honey," I say.

"I think I'll go on to bed," she says, not quite meeting my gaze. "All that cooking wore me out."

Sam sets down his coffee cup. "I should be going then."

"No," Kat says quickly. "Stay. It's nice for Mama to have someone to talk to."

I blush nine shades of red, say goodnight to my daughter, and wait until she's gone before saying, "I'm not sure what's worse. The overt matchmaking or the concession to how pitiful her mom's social life is."

"It's a compliment to me," Sam says. "I don't see her wanting you to spend time with just anyone."

"She never has before," I say, then realizing how revealing the statement is, I add, "Not often, I mean."

There's some silence, and then Sam says, "Are you seeing anyone?"

I laugh. I can't help it. "Well, if I am, he's not around much, is he?"

"I shouldn't have asked. It's none of my business."

"No, it isn't," I say. "But no, I'm not."

The emotion that flits across his face can only be described as relief, and something inside me startles at the realization. I feel us inching toward a tightrope, testing a toe to its tension, weighing the wisdom of walking its length.

I should turn and run, as fast and as far as I can go. Flight instinct dictates it. But the old pull is there. I feel it as strong as I've ever felt anything, the pulse of it taking up its former space inside me. I'm as powerless to resist now as I had been when I was too young to know better.

The night has come alive around us, voices in the dark beyond the deck calling out to one another, a hoot owl announcing its presence, a dog protesting its isolation.

And then there's the voice inside me, all but screaming to stop this craziness, turn back before it's too late. But I already know it is. Even as Sam sets his coffee cup on the deck railing, even before he reaches out and touches my face with the back of his hand. Even before the soft sigh of acquiescence slips past my lips.

Some things that you've thought about for a long time have a way of not living up to the hype you've given them. Sam's kiss isn't one of them. He takes his time with it, easing in until his lips settle on mine, and any reason I might have been able to come up with as to why this is a bad idea flies off into the night.

I slip my arms around his waist, and the feel of him is so familiar, it's as if nearly two dozen years instantly dissolve, and we are exactly as we once were, two people who simply fit one another.

The kiss is sweet, and, at the same time, full of fire.

Since the day he showed up at the dock, I've done a

decent job of concealing his effect on me. A person can alter the tone of their voice to hide emotion, school the expression on their face to show something other than longing. But not here. In his arms. Under the old magic of his kiss.

Here, I'm the very same girl who first fell in love with him. The same girl who wanted him beyond anything resembling reason. As I do now.

He runs a hand up the side of my bare arm, and electricity scatters throughout my body. His mouth finds the side of my neck, the hollow of my throat. I drop my head back and sigh with surrender.

"It's only felt this way once for me," he says against my throat. "Only with you, Gabby."

I want to make him stop, tell him not to say things that inspire regret in either of us. It does no good, after all. We can't go back and change any of it. But the truth is, I want to hear that he never forgot me, never forgot what it was like between us.

"For me too, Sam."

There, honesty. With all its pointy edges and potential pitfalls. But somehow it feels good to let it out, release it from that place inside me where I've forced it to hide for so long.

He leans back and stares down at me. I feel him drinking me in, like someone who's been too long without vital nutrients and only now realizes his need.

And this time, I kiss him. Pull his face to mine with open urgency.

We kiss with the kind of abandon I haven't known since we last made love, and I don't know whether that's tragically sad or simply wonderful that we've found it again.

At some point, he backs me to a nearby lounge chair, eases me down onto the cushion and then follows, stretching out alongside me. I yank his shirt from his pants and slip my hands up his back, splaying them across his shoulders. The muscles there are taut and firm, and I remember the breadth and strength of them.

Sam pulls my blouse from my jeans and slips his hand inside, finding the bareness of my waist and then the curve of my breast. All the while, we're kissing with a deliberation that can only lead to one conclusion, and it is this thought that brings common sense swooping to the front of my mind.

"Sam," I say, his name ragged on my lips. "Not here." I glance at the sliding glass doors, suddenly aware that Kat could come back out at any moment.

I sit up, drawing in a couple of deep, return-to-sanity breaths.

Sam runs a hand over my hair. "I'm sorry—"

"Don't be. It's just—I'm not ready—"

"It's okay." He slides to the end of the chair and sits for a few moments with his hands on his knees. I know he's forcing himself back to reason, and I keep my gaze on his back as his breathing slows.

Still not facing me, he reaches for my hand, linking his fingers through mine. "I never thought I would hold you like that again."

I know I shouldn't ask this. It feels like I'm asking him to admit to infidelity. But I can't help myself. "Did you think about us? Ever?"

"I'm not sure a day has ever passed that I didn't think about you, Gabby. I know what I lost, when I lost you. I'll never get that back. But I never stopped loving you. There were periods of time when I tried to convince myself that what I'd felt for you was just teenage love, and couldn't compare with the kind of love that adults with life experience come to know. And then at some point, I just let myself accept that the place in my heart where you had been would never be filled. And I was going to have to live with that."

I should feel some kind of vindication for the revelation, but I don't.

I find myself feeling simply grateful. To know again what we knew so long ago. To feel the petals of that love begin to peel back and lift their faces to the sun.

What we're going to do with it, I have no idea. It's at once fragile and sturdy, new and not new at all.

"I should go, Gabby," Sam says, standing. "Even though I don't want to."

"I don't want you to," I say, finding that I can't be anything but honest with him.

I get to my feet, and we stand for a moment. It no longer feels as if there's a canyon of distance between us. I feel the reconnect like a lock that has gently clicked back into place.

Sam reaches for my hand, laces his fingers between mine, but says nothing. He kisses my forehead, then releasing me altogether, walks to the sliding glass door and lets himself out. I wait a few moments until I know he's had time to leave the house and then go to the front living room window.

The light from the front porch allows me to see him clearly. He walks toward his car with purpose, as if he doesn't trust himself not to turn around and come back in. I can't help it. I wish that he would.

He comes to a sudden stop and puts a hand to the back of his head, and I watch him waiver, as if he's had too much to drink. A knot tenses in my stomach, and then he walks on, getting in his car and sitting for a moment, leaning his head against the seat.

Questions run through my mind all at once—Is he regretting what just happened between us?—Is something wrong?—Should I go out to check on him?

But he is starting the car and backing from the driveway before I can force my feet to move. I consider calling to ask if everything is okay, but I stop myself under a feeling I can't explain.

Kind of like when you're about to see something you don't want to see, and so you look away right before you have to process what it is. When you can't handle the reality of what it might be.

Anger is an acid that can do more harm to the vessel in which it is stored than to anything on which it is poured.

~ Mark Twain

Analise

I wake up with the kind of headache that feels as if every speck of moisture has been sucked from my brain.

I roll over and pull the pillow over my face in an attempt to block the sunlight streaming through the blinds of my room. I need to get up for class, but the thought of moving makes me instantly nauseous.

Helen lived up to her reputation and then some last night, getting us into a club on the outskirts of London, where we were over-served and then put in a taxi back to school when it was clear we weren't going to be able to hail one on our own.

It would be nice to think that the alcohol somehow managed to douse the anger that seems to be a permanent fixture inside me. But as soon as I think of Mom and our phone call yesterday, it's back to raging volume.

I swing my feet over the side of the bed, and the whole room seems to list. I so want to throw up.

My phone buzzes. I fumble for it and find it under the covers. It's a text from Evan.

Hey. What up?

I type back, my fingers quick.

Twenty four hours later. Is that the best you can do?

Ease up. Have a life here.

Everyone is gone.

What do you mean?

You're off doing your own thing. I'm here in this dungeon of a school. Mom's married to her yoga now. And Dad's in Virginia.

What?

At least he didn't tell you either.

When did he go?

A week or so ago.

Do you know why?

No.

Hmm.

Thanks for the in-depth analysis.

How long will he be there?

He said he wasn't sure.

That's weird.

Brainiac.

There's a b word I could throw back at you, but I won't.

Ever the gentleman.

If you're so miserable, you can come visit me in the city this weekend.

And hang out with your stodgy friends? No thanks.

I'm reconsidering the b word.

I just wish things were the way they used to be.

That we weren't all separated.

What? You don't even like being around Mom and Dad.

I liked having a family.

You still do.

Some family.

This time when it hits, the nausea isn't taking no for an answer. I bolt off the bed and run into the bathroom where I drape myself across the toilet and vomit until there is nothing left to throw up. And when I'm done, I don't know if I've ever felt so empty.

It is difficult to obtain the friendship of a cat. It is a philosophical animal... one that does not place its affections thoughtlessly.

~ Theophile Gautier

Sam

I sleep until noon the following day, the medicine I'd taken for my headache blocking my brain's normal alarm clock. When I come to, I feel groggy, but the pain is gone, and I lie in bed staring at the ceiling fan while memories of last night with Gabby come floating up.

I close my eyes and feel the imprint of her against me, the sweet smell of her hair, the softness of her mouth. She'd felt different in my arms in a way I don't know that I can explain, but at the same time, so much the same. I've never had that sense of belonging with anyone else, not before Gabby or after. I know I should feel guilty for the thought. During the years that Megan and I worked at our marriage, I wanted to give her all of me.

I tried.

But I know now that was never possible. A part of

me has always belonged to Gabby. It was never within my power to alter that, even though I honestly believed that I could.

From here, it seems so obvious, the impossibility of it. Like trying to alter the timing of a sunrise.

But even as I admit this to myself, guilt stirs up a sick feeling in my stomach. I have no right to start anything with Gabby.

I should leave. Just go to Baltimore and wait for Ben to get back. To do anything other than that makes me someone who could never deserve her.

I get out of bed and make my way to the shower, my steps tentative with the hope that my head will not start pounding again. Thankfully, it doesn't, and I stand under the cool shower spray with my eyes closed, knowing I have to leave this place that could so easily feel like home to me.

By the time I get downstairs and start to make some coffee, I am resigned to doing the right thing. I pick up my phone from the kitchen table, and it immediately rings.

The marina number flashes across the screen. I take a deep breath and answer with a neutral, "Good morning."

"Hi." Gabby's voice, hesitant, unsure. "How are you?"

"Good. You?"

"I just—I was wondering if you would be willing to go with Kat and me to Duke on Monday morning? We have the appointment with Dr. Lanning. Which I can't thank you enough for. And—"

"Gabby," I interrupt. "I would love to go with you, but I've been thinking, and last night—"

"You're regretting," she says.

"Who could ever regret kissing you?"

She doesn't say anything for several moments, and I'm wondering if I should have curbed the honesty when she says, "I don't regret kissing you, Sam."

I sit down on a kitchen chair and stare out the window at the lake beyond. I want to say yes. To be there for support even if I have little else to contribute. But I also know that the more I let our lives become entwined, the harder it will be to disentangle those threads again without immense pain.

"Sam, I'm not asking you to marry me. It's just a drive to North Carolina and back."

Her voice is light, as if she's trying to convince herself as well as me that the situation doesn't have to be complicated. Only she has no idea how complicated it really is.

But I give in to my own desire to be with her again, to see this appointment with David through. And so I say, "What time are we leaving?"

~

I SIT AT THE table, sipping coffee and skimming the *New York Times* on my iPad. And then even though I've told myself I'm not going to do it again, my fingers type in the search words as if on automatic pilot. I browse through the forums, reading the situations of a dozen different people who are facing the same future as I am.

I look for hope there, but as has been the case each and every time I've done this, I finally back out of the screen and close the device cover, wishing I'd never given in to the temptation.

I resolve yet again to wait for my brother's opinion. To trust in his expertise and the fact that I know he will be honest with me because we've never been anything other than that with each other. He will tell me the truth. And that is what I need to hear.

I sit for a while, reining my thoughts back to quiet from their temporary escape into panic.

I hear a sound at the back door off the kitchen. At first, I assume it's just the breeze brushing leaves against the screen, but then I hear it again. I walk to the door and pull it open.

Sitting on the welcome mat is a black cat. Something about its posture makes me think of what a cat belonging to a rich Egyptian in pyramid times might have looked like. It is as poised and regal as any cat that might have laid claim to Cleopatra.

That's my first impression. But a closer look reveals that its recent circumstances most certainly did not involve royal treatment of any kind.

"Hey, buddy," I say. "When was your last meal?"

The meow is instant and insistent, as if arriving on

my doorstep included the assumption that a meal would be forthcoming. "I can help you out with that. What happened to your ears?"

I squat down and see that the edges of both ears are bloody and infected. The cat stands tall on all fours and does a body swipe against my legs.

"I'll take that as a please," I say. "Come on in."

I step back inside, and the cat follows me, tail sticking straight in the air, as if its appearance might be tattered, but its dignity is intact.

I rummage through the pantry and find a can of chicken that Ben's family must have left here at some point. I check the expiration date. It's still good, so I pull a bowl from the cabinet and spoon the chicken in.

I set it on the floor, and the thank-you meows are nearly deafening.

"You're welcome," I say. "You could use some medicine on those ears, you know."

I search around until I find some cotton balls and hydrogen peroxide and then a tube of antibiotic ointment. I wait for the cat to finish its meal—which doesn't take long at all. I pick it up, checking to see if it's a boy or girl—boy—and then set him on the table.

He's surprisingly patient with my first-aid efforts, as if he knows his ears need the care. When I'm done, I run my hand along his back and he arches into the rub the way cats do.

"Now what?" I ask him.

Meow.

"Does that mean you want to hang a while?"

Meow.

"I'll take that as a yes. But I have to be up front with you. It can't be a permanent thing. So temporary lodging at best. That good with you?"

Me-owow.

"You have a name?"

Silence follows the question, but he rubs against my arm as if he's okay with me giving him one. "Okay. Let's see. Eli sound good?"

No response, so I'm not sure we're in agreement, but I guess we'll go with it.

Eli hops down from the table and charts a path for the living room. It's clear he's owned a home before. I follow him and stick my head inside the doorframe just as he jumps onto the couch and curls into a neat ball in one corner. He closes his eyes immediately, as if he's exhausted. I wonder if I'm actually being kind to let him stay when I know it can't be for long.

And then I realize I'm deliberating the same thing about the cat that I'm deliberating about Gabby.

A wave of fatigue hits me, and I decide I don't have the energy to question the rightness of anything that I'm doing.

"As long as I'm here, Eli, you can stay," I say and then leave him to his nap.

When one door of happiness closes, another opens;
but often we look so long at the closed door that we do
not see the one which has been opened for us.

~ Helen Keller

Gabby

I drive out to Annie's house Saturday afternoon, intent on delivering an apology, even as I'm not sure what I'm apologizing for. Possibly for being careless with my own emotions. In all fairness, I know that she has my best interests at heart.

She waves at me from the entrance to the big red barn as I pull into the driveway. I get out and walk down to where she's spreading feed to the chickens clucking at her feet.

"Hey," she says.

"Hey," I say, and then with my arms folded across my chest, "How many do you have now?"

"Fourteen," she says, tossing another handful of feed.

"You're getting eggs every day?"

"At least a dozen."

"That's nice."

"They earn their keep and then some. Haven't seen a mosquito in ages."

The chickens peck and dart, each one determined not to lose out. "Do they go in at night?"

"Yep. We built the coop behind the barn. They let themselves in every evening just before dark. By the time I come down to close them up, most of them are asleep."

"What made you decide to have chickens? Before you married Scott, you said the only animals you liked were dogs."

"People can change, Gabby," she says sharply.

"I'm sorry. I didn't mean that to be critical."

Annie sighs and slings another handful of chicken feed. "And I don't mean to be Mrs. Super Sensitive."

I smile at this and say, "It's okay. You're mad at me."

"I'm not mad at you."

"Yes, you are."

"Okay, I'm mad at you."

"You think I'm being stupid."

"If I'm honest."

"Can I throw some?" I ask, reaching out for the bag.

"Sure," she says, opening the top.

I scatter some of the feed and several chickens go after it with admirable determination. "Logically, I know you're right, Annie. And I know you saw me at my worst."

"That I did."

"But like you said, people change."

"And you forgive him? Just like that?" she asks, snapping her fingers.

"I can't explain it, Annie. If you had asked me a month ago, I would have said you were crazy."

Annie puts the bag of feed away just inside the barn and says, "Come on, I'll make you a glass of iced tea. I'm thirsty."

We walk to the house in silence, but it's the kind between old friends where words aren't always necessary. I wait on the front porch while she goes in the house. The swing plays its own squeaky song. Looking out across the green pastures of this farm, I can see why Annie loves everything about it.

She's back in a couple of minutes with two delicious glasses of iced tea, mint fresh from her herb garden floating in between the ice cubes. "Thank you," I say.

She sits down next to me, takes a sip and then says, "You know my only care is that you don't get hurt again."

"I know. That's why you're my friend."

"I don't feel much like a friend at the moment. I feel more like the chastising parent."

"Because you want to protect me. That's what good parents do."

"Except you're not going to listen to me."

"I want to. I just don't know if I can."

"Can you not remember all the pain you went through when he—"

"I can. I do."

She sighs and pushes the swing back with her feet, and we glide gently back and forth. "Well, if that's not enough of a deterrent, there's nothing I can come up with to beat it."

I reach across and put my hand over hers. "I don't know what's going to happen, Annie. I just can't make myself close the door yet."

"Fair enough," she says. "I'll be here."

And I know that what she hasn't said is as meaningful as what she has.

She'll be here. To pick up the pieces.

The best things in life are unexpected – because
there were no expectations.
~ Eli Khamarov

Gabby

I don't hear anything from Sam on Sunday, and it seems as if it takes forever for Monday morning to arrive. The appointment is at nine o'clock, and since the drive will take two-and-a-half hours, we pick Sam up at 6:15.

He's waiting outside when we pull into the driveway. Sitting next to him like a small sentry is a black cat. He reaches down and rubs the cat's head before walking out to the car and sliding in.

"Morning," he says, not quite meeting my gaze and smiling at Kat in the back.

"Good morning," the two of us say in unison.

"Do you have a cat, Sam?" Kat asks.

"I have a boarder," he says. "He arrived on Saturday, and we've worked out a temporary arrangement."

I smile at this and say, "Does he know it's temporary?"

"I was quite clear about the terms of our contract."

Kat laughs. "Will he be outside while we're gone?"

"I propped the screen porch door open so he can go in and out."

"He looks as if he's right at home," I say.

"What's his name?" Kat asks.

"Eli. Or at least while he's here."

"What will happen to him when you leave?"

"I don't know," Sam says. "We haven't gotten that far."

"We could come over and feed him when you're not here."

Sam hesitates, and then, "That's a really nice offer, Kat."

"I like cats," she says. "They have a good name."

Sam and I both chuckle at this. In a few minutes, Kat puts her ear plugs in to listen to music. It's only then that I say, "Thank you for coming with us."

"I'm glad to," he says.

I find myself gripping the steering wheel a little tighter when I add, "I don't expect anything, Sam. Just so you know."

"I know you don't. But you have every right to."

"Just not from you?"

"I wish it could be me."

"I don't know what to make of that."

"And I don't know how to explain it."

"Stalemate?"

"Stalemate."

We drive in silence for a good bit, and then I finally say, "Can we just let this be whatever it can be for however long it can be?"

He looks over at me, and I glance at him long enough to see the look of longing in his eyes. I know he wants this as much as I want it, but whatever is holding him back is bigger than my desire or his.

"I don't want to hurt you, Gabby," he says softly.

"I'm not going to let you," I say, my voice exuding a confidence I'm not sure is real.

He stares out the window for a mile or two, his jaw tight. But when he looks at me, his expression has lost its storminess. And there is resignation in his voice when he says, "Okay. We'll let it be whatever it is, for as long as it is."

I feel complete relief in hearing it, and I force myself not to look beneath the surface of his concession, even though the tiniest voice tells me I should.

The first wealth is health.

~ Ralph Waldo Emerson

Sam

David has barely changed. He was a runner in college, and he still has the same lean build he had then. A bit less hair but other than that, he's pretty much the same.

We greet each other in his office with backslapping and man-hugs. Gabby and Kat stand back and watch with small smiles on their faces, as if they are surprised to see that we know each other this well.

David steps away and clears his throat, extending a hand to Gabby. "I'm David. Dr. Lanning," he corrects.

"Hello," Gabby says. "This is my daughter, Kat."

"Hello," Kat says from her chair, suddenly shy.

"I hope you'll excuse Sam and me," he says. "We were good buddies in med school. It's been a long time."

"It has," I agree.

"I hope we'll have a few minutes to catch up before you go," David says.

"Yes," I say. "And we're here about Kat, of course."

"Please, sit," Dr. Lanning directs us. "Let's get a bit of history if we can."

I look at Gabby and say, "I can wait outside while you—"

"We'd like for you to stay," she says.

I take the chair next to hers.

"How old are you, Kat?" David asks, looking at her with a smile in his eyes.

"I'm ten," she says with all the pride the age deserves.

"Ten is outstanding," he says. "I've looked at the chart, Ms.—"

"Gabby," she interjects.

"Gabby," he says. "So I have a good idea of the back story. Was there any particular incident that triggered Kat's current pain?"

"We don't think so. It started out as a nagging kind of thing and then continued to increase. It's most noticeable when she stands or walks."

"Hmm," he says, making notes in her file. "I would like to start with a physical exam and an MRI."

David picks up his phone and asks for a nurse to show us to the exam room. She's there in seconds, smiling a greeting and helping Kat with her chair.

Gabby follows the nurse out of the office, turning to say, "Thank you, Sam. And thank you, Dr. Lanning."

"You're most welcome," David says. "See you in a few minutes."

~

ONCE GABBY AND KAT leave the room, David leans back in his chair, looks at me and says, "It's good to see you, old friend."

"It's good to see you, David."

"May I be nosy?"

"Sure."

"Are you and Megan still together?"

"No," I say, sitting up and leaning forward with my elbows on my knees. "We've been divorced a little over a year."

"I'm sorry," he says. "Sucks, doesn't it?"

"You too?"

"Unfortunately."

We shake our heads, and then David says, "Are you and Gabby—"

"We used to be."

"Ah."

"In high school."

"Wow."

"Yeah."

"Have you moved back from England?"

"No. I don't know. I'm not sure."

"Kids are still there?"

"Yes."

"That makes it tough. Is Gabby part of the reason you'd like to stay?"

"It's complicated," I say.

We sit for a stretch of moments, before David says, "Are you okay, Sam?"

"Yeah," I say, trying to force a lightness I don't feel into my voice.

"May I be honest?"

"Of course."

"You don't look exactly well."

I absorb what he's said, start to brush it off with a light reply, but I truly can't force myself to do it. Instead, I look down and say, "I always knew you would be a good doctor."

"What is it, Sam?"

And I find myself telling him, this friend I haven't seen in years. I watch his face as he absorbs each word, and by the time I'm done, David's expression tells me all I need to know.

Sometimes it's better to put love into hugs than to put it into words.

~ Author Unknown

Gabby

Dr. Lanning conducts his physical exam of Kat with a professional persona that feels a little different from the less-serious version of himself we met in his office a short while ago.

I've often wondered how doctors handle the difference between seeing people as people and people as patients. I guess it must be critical, this ability to slip a shield into place when objectivity isn't optional.

I sit in silence on the chair next to the exam table, my hands clasped in my lap. My heart pounds with anxiety. For me, this has been the hardest part of being Kat's mother. Not the fact that she has this condition that will be with her for the rest of her life, but that I wish I could take her pain and discomfort on myself.

I would rather feel the fear and uncertainty than know that she is feeling it. She's brave. She's always been brave. But I can see in the set of her jaw and unsmiling eyes that she is worried.

She has seen so many doctors in her young life, some of the experiences less than pleasant. I steel myself not to reach for her hand, but can hardly wait until he is done and I can pull her into my arms for a hug.

"Could you lie flat on your belly for me, Kat?" Dr. Lanning asks.

She does so, and he parts the back of the paper gown to run his hands gently along her spine. She winces at one point, and he says, "I'm sorry, Kat. Is that where the pain is?"

She nods, biting her lower lip.

"Okay. You can sit back up."

Dr. Lanning looks at me and says, "I've already set up the MRI. It should only be twenty or thirty minutes before they take you down for that. Would you like to just wait here?"

"That's fine," I say. "Thank you so much."

"Thank you for being so patient with me, Kat. These pictures we're going to take next will give me a better idea of how to address what's going on here. Sound good?"

"Yes, sir," she says.

"I'll see you in a bit then." He leaves the room, closing the door behind him.

"Are you okay, Mama?" Kat asks, once he's gone.

"Yes, sweetie," I say, standing. "But I'd really like to give you a hug."

"I'd really like for you to," she says, opening her arms to me.

You don't really understand human nature unless you know why a child on a merry-go-round will wave at his parents every time around — and why his parents will always wave back.

~ **William D. Tammeus**

sam

I'm waiting in the lobby off the X-ray department when a nurse wheels Kat down the hallway. Gabby is right behind them, and from the look on her face, I can tell she's trying to be brave.

"Okay, Mom," the nurse says when they reach the set of double doors marked MRI. "If you can please wait right here, I'll have her back to you in no time. That all right with you, young lady?" she adds to Kat.

Kat nods, trying to smile, but it wavers a bit. Tears pop into Gabby's eyes.

She stands with her arms folded across her chest, staring at the doors through which the nurse has just disappeared with Kat. Her shoulders are shaking a little.

I walk over and put a hand on her arm, saying, "It's gonna be okay. But I know. It's awful when it's them, isn't it?"

She nods, biting her lower lip.

"Come on," I say. "Let's sit down."

Gabby follows me, and we take the two chairs in the far corner of the room away from the annoying TV hanging on one wall.

"When Evan was seven years old," I say, "he was spending the night with a friend from school. The boy's mother picked him up on a Saturday morning early because they had planned to go to a soccer tournament an hour or so away. A car driving the wrong way on the freeway hit them head on at eighty miles an hour. The driver was drunk. Evan's friend and his mother were both killed. They were in the front seats. Evan was in the back.

"He was in the ICU for a month. For a lot of that time, we had no idea whether he would live or not. The doctors didn't give us a lot of hope. I can honestly say I would have given anything to change places with him. Seeing him in that bed hooked up to tubes and IVs like this shell of his vibrant self—it was nearly unbearable."

Gabby's grip tightens, and her eyes are filled with sympathy when she says, "Oh, Sam. My gosh. I'm so sorry."

"Thanks," I say. "It's not something you would wish on anyone."

"How did you get through it?"

"I spent a lot of time on my knees," I say.

She nods, squeezing my hand. "Sometimes, that's the

only place to go. Is he okay now? I mean, were there any lasting effects?"

"No. Miraculously, there's no evidence that it ever happened. It was as if he had stayed in the coma until his body healed what was broken. I can't explain it. I met other parents during that time who had children with serious injuries, and, of course I met many in my practice over the years. I think there's a universal dread among those of us who love our children the way parents are supposed to love their children."

"That we would rather be the one suffering than to see them suffer," Gabby says softly.

I pull her into my arms and wrap her up against me, wanting to comfort her in the way I know she needs comforting. She presses her face to my chest. I feel the moisture of her tears, rubbing a hand over the back of her hair. "She's going to be all right."

"I just want this to be fixed for her. I want her to be a regular little girl who gets to run and play. I know her disease is never going to go away, but for her to be in pain so much of the time is—"

"David is a great doctor," I finish for her.

Gabby nods, her face still against me. I press my lips to the top of her head before I let myself consider the wisdom of it. She looks up at me with raw honesty in her eyes. I can't deny what I see there. I don't want to deny it, and I don't want to hide what I'm feeling from her either. "Gabby," I say.

She presses a finger to my lips and says, "Shh. Is there anything wrong with us comforting each other?"

I shake my head, and pull her close in against me. We wait like that until the nurse sticks her head through the swinging doors to let us know that they're all done.

Honest hearts produce honest actions.

~ Brigham Young

Gabby

Kat is asleep in the back seat before we're even out of Durham. Her fatigue tells me that the morning had been as stressful for her as I had thought. She usually has so much energy at this time of the day.

"How long do you think it will be before Dr. Lanning lets us know something?" I ask, glancing at Sam.

"Knowing David, I feel sure he'll call you as soon as they get the results."

"I really don't know how to thank you, Sam, for making all of this happen."

"You don't need to."

"But I want to. Can you come over for supper tonight?"

"It's not necessary, Gabby."

"It won't be Kat's level of cooking."

He looks at me with a smile. "She's a tough act to follow."

"I'm not promising I won't ask for her help."

"We're on," he says.

~

WE DROP SAM OFF at his house just before three o'clock. Eli, the cat, is waiting on the front-door step, as if he's been sitting there since we left this morning.

Sam scoops him up and brings him over to the car where Kat can pet him through the window. Eli allows the small show of worship as if it's his due.

On the way home, Kat reviews her list of reasons for why we need to get a dog or cat. It's been a year since Sawyer, our yellow lab, passed away. I just haven't had the heart to let anyone take his place. But I realize it's probably time to do so for Kat. I know how much she misses his company.

"We'll work on that," I say.

Kat is so excited she can barely sit still the rest of the drive. She recites off boy and girl name possibilities as if she's been rehearsing for months.

I ask Kat what she thinks I should fix for supper. She pulls out her favorite cookbook, a country Italian tome that Myrtle gave her for Christmas last year. She begins making suggestions. I flip through the pages with her, letting her decide which of the recipes are worth making tonight.

"These might be a little above my pay grade," I say.

She giggles. "I'll help you, Mama."

We spend a full three hours in the kitchen, and I think we use every pot and frying pan we own. The wonderful smell of butter and onion sautéing in the skillet fills the room, and I realize how wonderful it is to be able to share times like this with my daughter.

I suppose I'm the one who should be teaching, but instead, I'm the one learning from her.

We've just stuck the pasta in the oven to bake when Kat looks at me and says, "Would it be all right if I watch a movie and eat my supper in the living room?"

I lean back and raise an eyebrow. "Are you doing the matchmaking thing again? If so, you don't need to do that."

"I know. I just think it would be nice if you had like, you know, a real date."

"Honey," I say carefully. "It's not really a date."

"Are you saying you two don't like each other?"

"No. We do like each other."

"Then why can't it be a date?"

"Sweetie, it's really complicated."

"Which is code for what adults say when they're about to make a mess of something."

"You are way too smart to be ten years old, you know that?"

"It just seems to me that if both of you like each other, it really shouldn't be complicated."

"In a perfect world, I guess it wouldn't be," I say.

"But we don't live in a perfect world," she says.

"No, we don't. So we kind of have to make the best of things, right?"

"Right," I say.

"Okay. I'm going to eat my supper in the living room and watch a movie."

I know my daughter. There's no point in arguing.

Perhaps I am stronger than I think.

~ Thomas Merton

Gabby

We decide to take the walk before dessert.

I check in with Kat to make sure she's all right with her movie. She teases me by making a kissing sound when she waves.

Outside the house, the night is dark under the overcast sky. Clouds had moved in late that afternoon, a ceiling beneath the stars. Low mushroom lights direct us along the stone walkway to the dock.

We walk there in silence, reaching the end where I take off my sandals and sit down to dangle my feet in the water. Sam takes off his running shoes, rolls up the bottoms of his jeans and sits down next to me.

"It's amazingly warm," he says.

"It is." I run my fingers through the water, flick some at him.

"Hey," he says, and splashes me back.

I laugh. "Do you remember that time we got caught out in a thunderstorm on the boat?"

"You mean the one where I thought we were going to die?"

"Yes. That one," I say. "I thought the waves were going to come inside the boat."

"I think they might have, if we hadn't gotten to a dock and taken shelter under the porch of that house."

"Thank goodness the owners weren't home."

"I felt bad for having you out there," Sam says. "You kept telling me the storm was coming, but I wanted to ski just one more time."

"Me the pessimist. You the optimist."

"Probably more like you were the smart one and I was the dumb one."

I laugh. "Hardly." We sit quiet for a few moments while a boat hums by somewhere out on the lake beyond us.

"Do you ever wonder why those memories are so easy to pull up? I mean honestly, there are things that happened to me three years ago that I don't remember. Places I've visited that I barely remember what I did there."

"I don't know," I say. "Maybe because they were some of our firsts."

"Is it like that for you?" he asks.

I don't hesitate. "Yes."

"Things seemed so simple then."

"They were simple. Because it was just you and me and what we felt for each other." My hands are clasped at the edges of the dock. Sam reaches out and presses his hand over mine. We sit, quiet, just absorbing the connection. I turn my palm up and link my fingers with his.

"I know you don't want this now," I say. "But it's still there, isn't it?"

"It is," he says. "And it isn't that I don't want it, Gabby. That I don't want you. Dear God, I do."

"Then, why?" I ask, hearing the broken note in my own voice.

He makes a sound of surrender and reaches for me, lifting me up and onto his lap so that my legs are straddling his, and we are chest to chest, our faces nearly touching. I tip my forehead against his, draw in a shallow breath, then brush his lips with mine.

He kisses me back, softly, but I feel the longing in him. I deepen the kiss. I loop my arms around his neck and remember the night so long ago when we had given ourselves to each other. It seems like a lifetime behind us, and, at the same time, a mere blink. I remember what it felt like to be his, to be one with him. And there is nothing I want more than to know that closeness again.

I don't know how long we kiss like that, but it's a long time. And when Sam drops back onto the dock, his arms above his head, as if in surrender, I stretch out on top of him, looking down into his face.

"I want you so much," I say.

"I want you too," he says.

"Just not now."

"Just not now," he repeats.

"Will there ever be a now?"

"I want to believe so," he says. "More than anything, I want to believe so."

I need for him to explain to me why it can't be now, but, for whatever reason, I know that he can't.

"The possibility of a now," I say, "I can live with that."

"I don't deserve your waiting, Gabby."

"Will you let me be the one to decide that?" I ask, leaning down to kiss the corner of his mouth.

"Only because I'm a selfish jerk," he says.

"That's not how I see it," I say.

Sam puts a hand to the side of his head and closes his eyes, pain flashing across his face.

"What is it?" I ask. "What's wrong?"

I slide off him. He tries to sit up, then falls back onto one elbow, his face still contorted with pain.

"Sam," I say, my voice a harsh cry. I get to my feet and reach to help him up. "What's wrong?"

"I—it's just a bad headache," he says.

"Let me help you." I put an arm around his waist. "Let's go back to the house. I have some medicine there." My heart is beating so hard I can feel it pounding against my chest.

He starts to say something, but his jaw clenches again, and he squeezes his eyes shut.

"Sam. You're scaring me. Please, let's go to the house."

He leans on me a bit, and we walk slowly along the dock. I feel more of his weight settle onto my shoulder, and then he starts to fall.

I grab hold of him, trying to wrap my arms around his waist, but I'm not quick enough, and we're right at the edge of the dock. And then we're both falling, off the side, down, down. It seems like forever before we hit the surface of the water. Just as we do, I feel Sam go completely limp, and realize he's passed out.

My scream is instant and piercing, even to my own ears. "Sam! Sam!" But I've lost my grip on him. He's sinking into the night-dark water. "No! Sam!"

I reach below the surface, trying to grab onto him and pull him back to me. I don't know how deep the water is here, but I can't touch the bottom. I flail about, finally grabbing onto the back of his shirt. His weight pulls me down, and I take in a mouthful of water, just as my head slips beneath the surface.

Time flies over us, but leaves its shadow behind.

~ Nathaniel Hawthorne

Gabby

I can swim. I had many lessons as a child. But I've never considered myself a strong swimmer. Fear threatens to consume my rational brain, and I have to steel myself not to let it overcome me. I know I can't let go of Sam, because in the dark water, I will never be able to find him again in time.

And so, with my lungs screaming for relief, I hold onto his shirt with both hands and start to kick with my legs in the direction I pray is the shore.

I don't know how long it takes me to reach the point where I can stand on the bottom of the lake, my head breaking through the surface, my lungs begging for air.

I breathe in great chunks of it, gasping and sputtering, but never letting go of Sam.

He's still face down. I have to get him to the edge of the water. My arms feel as if they are going to snap from the pressure of his weight. But somehow, I manage to get him in close enough that the upper half of his body is flat on the sandy shore. I struggle to turn him over onto his back, calling out his name over and over again. "Sam! Sam, please! Wake up!"

I begin screaming for Kat as I struggle to remember the basics of the CPR class I took when I first brought her home. I force myself to draw in a calming breath and then begin pumping his chest, alternating with breathing into his mouth.

"What is it, Mama?" I hear Kat call out from the deck at the house. "What's wrong?"

"Call 911! It's Sam. He needs help. As fast as you can, honey!"

I continue with the CPR, crying now with no ability whatsoever to stop my sobbing. "You cannot do this, Sam. You cannot do this. We haven't had our now. Don't go. Don't go."

I force another breath of air into his mouth, and suddenly he coughs, water flooding from his lungs.

"Oh, thank God," I say, crying harder. "Sam. Sam."

He opens his eyes, struggling for a moment to focus, and then he looks directly at me. "I'm sorry, Gabby. I'm so sorry."

Do the thing you think you cannot do.

~ Eleanor Roosevelt

Kat

I've never been this scared in my life.

Sam's face is so pale. Mama is rubbing his hair and crying softly. She's trying not to, but she can't help it. She's shaking, and I don't know if it's from being wet or because she's so scared too. Tears run down my face, and I reach out to put a hand on her shoulder.

The rescue squad sirens scream in the distance, and I'm so relieved they're almost here that my knees go weak.

"I told them to come to the dock, Mama," I say, my voice cracking with fear.

She nods and says, "Thank you, sweetie. Everything is going to be all right."

I want to believe this, and I know she does too. But something is awfully wrong with Sam. What if they can't fix it?

A flashlight beams across us. Two people from the rescue squad are running through the yard toward us, carrying a stretcher and a big bag.

"Here!" Mama cries out.

The man and woman get to work immediately, pulling out equipment and checking Sam's heartbeat.

"Can you tell us what happened, ma'am?" the man asks, his face serious.

Mama tells them how Sam collapsed and fell into the water. And how he started to sink and she pulled him in to the shore. I realize then just how brave she had to be to do that, how dark the water must have been down there. I reach out and take Mama's hand, holding on tight. I won't let go until she asks me to.

And then you find yourself living what you never imagined.

~ Author Unknown

Gabby

One of the paramedics asks me for as much information about Sam as I can give her. Insurance info? I find a card in his wallet. Previous medical history? I don't know.

The two of us follow the paramedics to the vehicle, its red lights still flashing in circles across the front yard of the house. I want to ride in the ambulance with him, but I'm soaking wet, and I can't leave Kat here alone.

They load the stretcher into the rescue squad, the woman paramedic climbing into the back with Sam. The other one slams the doors closed and looks at me. "We're taking him to Roanoke Memorial."

"We'll be there as quickly as possible."

He runs to the driver's side, jumps in, and the vehicle screams out of the driveway. The sound echoes in my heart.

~

I CHANGE MY clothes as quickly as I can. Kat is already waiting in the car when I run back out. She's even managed to get her wheelchair in the back by herself.

The drive to Roanoke seems as if it will take forever. I take the back way over Windy Gap Mountain because it comes out closest to the hospital near downtown.

My hands grip the steering wheel, and I stare straight ahead, pushing the curves as much as I dare.

"Can I say a prayer for Sam, Mama?" Kat asks from the back seat.

"Please, sweetie," I say.

I listen to the words, her soft pleas for Sam's safety, her quiet faith that her prayers will be answered.

The tears roll up and out of me with fresh force. I am struck with the feeling of still being in the water, knowing I'm being dragged down, even as I flail for the surface.

~

WE ARRIVE IN THE lobby off the emergency room, and when I ask for information about Sam, the woman at the front desk asks if I'm a relative.

"A friend," I answer.

She gives me a sympathetic smile, but says, "I'm sorry, ma'am, but we can't give information out to non-relatives."

"But we're the only people he knows here, and—"

"Again, I'm sorry. As soon as we are able to get Dr. Tatum's consent, we will let you know."

I roll Kat's chair across the lobby and take a seat on an empty row. My chest feels so tight that I can't get a deep breath.

Kat puts her hand on mine and says, "Don't they understand that he would feel better seeing us?"

"I'm sure they're just trying to protect their patients," I say, but I feel the same frustration as she does. And then I wonder if I should try to call his brother, someone in his family. Of course, I don't have any of their numbers or any idea of how to get in touch with them. But then I remember that Sam said Ben is in Hawaii, speaking at a conference.

I pull my phone from my purse, Google Ben's name, Hawaii, speaker, conference. The search wheel spins for a moment, and then the results pop onto the screen. A page on the Johns Hopkins website has a photo of Ben and a mention of the conference he is speaking at. The location is the Four Seasons Resort Hualalai.

I type the name into the search bar, and the hotel's website pops up as the first choice. I click and find the main number.

"I'm going to step outside and make a call, Kat."

She closes the book on her lap and says, "Want me to come?"

"No, sweetie. I'll be right back."

~

I ACTUALLY HAVE no idea what time it is in Hawaii right now. Are they three hours behind us? Five?

The hotel operator answers, and I ask to be connected with Ben Tatum's room.

"One moment, please," she says in a smooth voice.

"Thank you. Can you tell me what time it is there, please?"

"It's five-thirty a.m., ma'am."

"Thank you." Hopefully, that means he will be in the room.

The line rings four times before it clicks, and a groggy voice says, "Hello?"

"Ben," I say, trying to keep my words steady. "This is Gabby Hayden."

I wait for several seconds for him to process this. I've woken him, and he hasn't seen me in twenty-five years. I hardly expect him to recognize my name right off the bat.

"Gabby. What—is something wrong?"

"I'm afraid so, Ben. It's Sam. He collapsed tonight at my house. We're at the emergency room at Roanoke Memorial."

"What happened?" he asks. I hear the note of apprehension beneath the words and the fact that he is now fully awake.

"I'm not sure. I can't get any more information because they will only release it to relatives."

"Is there someone I can speak with?"

"It might be best if you call the hospital and see what you can find out."

"Of course. Can you give me your number, and I will call you back?"

"Yes."

"Just a moment. Let me grab a pen."

His tone is now neutral, and I suspect he is responding as a doctor intent on helping a patient.

"Okay," he says.

I give him the number and say, "Could you please let me know something as soon as you can? My daughter and I are here at the hospital. I won't leave until I know how he is."

"Gabby. Thank you. It's good to know that you're there with him."

I hear the dozen questions beneath his gratitude. Why was he with me? Are we together? But he says none of them, and we hang up with heavy goodbyes.

I go back inside then, take my seat beside Kat. I keep my phone in my hand, waiting for it to ring.

~

KAT HAS FALLEN asleep with her head in my lap when it finally does light up beneath the ringtone at just after three a.m. The screen says "unknown caller," and I close my eyes as I answer.

"It's Ben, Gabby. I'm sorry for how long this has taken."

Something in my stomach clenches at the tone of his

voice. His words sound as if they are each attached to weights.

"Did you learn anything?" I ask carefully.

I hear him draw in a deep breath and release it slowly. "I'm afraid it's not good," he says, and he can barely get the words out.

"What? What is it, Ben?"

He tries to answer, but the words break off. Finally, he manages, "Sam . . . he has a brain tumor, Gabby."

I don't know what I had expected him to say, but I am sure I have heard him wrong. "But that can't be. He's healthy and fit and—"

"I know," Ben says, tears still wavering through his voice.

"But . . . how bad is it?"

"From the CAT scan results they did tonight, it's not good. I was able to speak to his doctor in London. The tumor has grown since his last scan there. Which explains his pain and passing out earlier."

I try to process the words, but it's as if they are boulders I'm trying to filter through a sieve. "What do we do?" I ask, broken.

"I'm catching the next available flight there. I've asked the hospital to keep him comfortable, so he will be heavily sedated. I've also instructed them to add you and your daughter to the visitor's list."

"Thank you," I say, numb.

"Will you call me if anything changes? Anything at all?"

"Of course. And what about his family? His son and daughter, I mean?"

"I'll let them know. Thank you, Gabby. See you soon."

I end the call, but don't move, as if I have been turned to stone. I don't know what to think, what to feel. I just know I can't see him. Can't face him. If he wakes up, how can I possibly keep the grief from my eyes?

I move then, running back into the waiting area and gently shaking Kat awake. "We need to leave, honey."

She rubs her eyes and looks at me, her voice hoarse with sleep. "But we haven't seen Sam yet."

"I know, sweetie. We just need to get home, okay?"

"But no one else is here for him," she says, tears welling up.

"I'll call in the morning," I say, pushing her through the double doors.

I help her into the car and then get behind the wheel. My chest feels as if it is going to explode with a horrible mix of anger and sadness. I can barely swallow, and tears blur my vision as I pull out of the parking lot.

"I don't understand, Mama," Kat says, the words a little accusing.

"I know, sweetie. Neither do I."

~

AS SOON AS WE get home, I help Kat to her bed. She's so tired she can't hold her eyes open. We don't bother with her pajamas. She just slides under the covers. I pull the blankets up around her, kiss her forehead and leave the room, closing the door quietly behind me.

It's five-thirty in the morning, and sleep is the last thing I can think about. I go in my room and change into shorts and a T-shirt, and then put on my running shoes.

I let myself out of the house just as the sun starts to peek up from behind Smith Mountain. I start to run, as hard as I can, the sprint straining my lungs until it feels as if they are screaming inside me.

I run along the edge of the state road, grateful there are no cars this early. When the tears come, they geyser up and out of me, streaming down my face and blending with the sweat on my face. I am sobbing outright now, but I keep running. I can't stop. If I do, I am sure I will drown in the sorrow coming out of me.

I run until I physically give out, stumbling and falling onto the grass at the side of the road. I pull my legs up against my chest, my arm over my face. And I cry until there isn't a single tear left inside me.

There was another time in my life when I cried like this for Sam. When I thought I had lost him forever. I wonder now if I always had some small ray of hope that we might one day be together again. As horrible as that time had been, as grief-stricken as I was, that had been nothing compared to this.

If we could, I would go back, live through all that again even with no hope of me ever seeing him. Because he would still be in this world. And I could live with that.

But this? A world without Sam anywhere in it? I cannot imagine.

Bad dreams are fears gasping for breath.
~ Author Unknown

Kat

I see Mama falling. It's some kind of ledge, and I'm running to her, as fast as my legs will move. But I'm not quick enough. She's slipping from the edge, dropping off into empty space.

I scream her name over and over again, waking up and jerking upright in my bed. I am sweating, and my pajamas are sticking to me. "Mama!" I scream.

The house is quiet, but there's light coming through my curtains.

"Mama!" I call out again, jumping out of bed and instantly feeling the snap of pain in my back.

I press my hand to it, half-limping to the kitchen and not finding her there. I hurry through the rest of the house, but she's not here. I think about the hospital, Sam and what happened to him last night. Mama wouldn't tell me, but I know something is horribly wrong. And I don't know how that can be because he looks so healthy, like there couldn't possibly be anything wrong with him.

But that's how we lose people. They can be fine one minute. And gone from our life the next. When I was in the first grade, there was a girl named Cassie in my class whose mama got sick. When she went to the doctor, they told her she had three months to live. She didn't even live that long, and Cassie had to go and live with her grandmother in Kentucky.

After that, I didn't want to go to regular school anymore. I wanted to be at home with Mama where I could make sure nothing happened to her.

I don't want to be left. I don't want to be alone.

"Mama!" I call out again. When there's no answer, I sit down on the living room couch and start to cry.

We all need each other.

~ Leo Buscaglia

Gabby

I walk back. My legs feel as if they have been turned to lead, and it takes me a while to get back to the house. When I reach my driveway, I see Annie's car parked at an angle, the driver's side door open.

Fear grips my chest, and I run to the door, calling out, "Kat? Annie?"

"We're in here, Mama," Kat calls from the kitchen.

She's sitting at the table next to Annie, and I can see that she's been crying.

"What is it? Did something happen?"

"I woke up and you weren't here. I got worried that something happened to you like what happened to Sam."

"Oh, honey," I say, walking over to drop onto my knees in front of her. "I'm sorry. I'm fine. I went for a run. I didn't mean to scare you."

"I knew you were upset," she says, wiping the back of her hand across her eyes. "I don't want to lose you."

I put my arms around her and hug her tight.

Annie smooths her hand over the back of my hair and says, "Oh, Gabby. Kat told me what happened. I'm so sorry."

I squeeze my eyes shut and struggle for composure. "You did warn me, didn't you? That I would get my heart broken again."

Annie leans back a bit, as if I have struck her. "Gabby. This isn't the same. I never—"

I start to sob then. No matter how hard I try to hold it back, grief and anger and outrage boil up from deep inside me, spilling out in a flood of fresh tears.

Annie leans in, putting her arms around Kat and me, encircling us with love and compassion. "How could this happen, Annie?"

"Oh, Gabby. I don't know why bad things like this happen to people who surely don't deserve it."

"He's young. Forty-two."

"I know."

I open my mouth to say more, and then press my lips together. How many other people have I known who have had tragedy in their lives? People who tried to live right, be kind, give back to the world more than they took. Fair isn't a word that applies to our existence here. It's not a word that applies to my love for Sam. Our timing has never aligned with the realities of our lives.

"What can I do, Gabby?" Annie asks softly.

I stand. "Let me get Kat back to bed for a bit. Maybe you could make some coffee?"

"I could use some myself," Annie says.

~

ANNIE IS POURING coffee into two mugs on the table when I walk back into the kitchen.

"Sit," she says. "And drink."

"Thank you," I say, pulling out a chair and forcing myself to take a sip of the coffee.

"What are you going to do?" Annie asks quietly.

"I can't go back to the hospital. I can't see him like that."

"Kat said his brother, Ben, is on the way. How long before he gets here?"

"I don't know," I say, shaking my head.

"So no one is there with him?"

"No."

Annie reaches out and covers my hand with hers. "I know you're scared for him, for what you feel for him. But you need me to be your friend right now, so I'm going to be. If you don't go there and be with him, and something happens, you will never forgive yourself, Gabby. I know you. And I know this."

I stare at our joined hands while fear thrashes around inside me. "We just found each other again, Annie."

"I know, honey. And he's going to need you."

"When he collapsed, he fell into the lake. I didn't

think I was going to be able to save him, Annie. He just kept going down and down and—"

"You saved his life. That can't be for nothing."

I know she's right. I have to go back. As terrified as I am to face what I will find there, I have to see him.

"Can you take Kat home with you when she wakes up?"

"Sure I can. Do you want me to come to the hospital?"

"I think I need to do this by myself. Thank you, Annie."

"Don't shut me out, okay? I want to be here for you. You need me to be here for you."

I lean over and give her a hug, more thankful for her friendship than ever.

If we had known the path, would we still have taken it?

~ Author Unknown

Sam

I hear people coming and going around me. Soft shoes, hushed voices, the disinfectant smell I recognize so well.

I'm in the hospital. I try to open my eyes, but it's as if they've been sealed shut, and I'm a prisoner behind them. I want to call out to whoever is in the room, but I can't force any words through my lips.

My memory struggles to grab onto something. I can't figure out what.

And then Gabby's face flashes through my groggy thoughts. I hear her voice screaming my name over and over again. I remember falling into the water and then the instant blackness. Waking up on the shore with Gabby over me, looking down at me with frantic eyes.

I realize then that she pulled me out of the water. Kept me from drowning. She saved my life.

And for what?

I wonder if it would have been better for us all if she had let me go, if she had just let me drown.

By now, she must know. I can hardly bear the thought that I have broken her heart not once in our lives, but twice.

I feel the tears slip through my closed eyes and slide down my face. I cannot lift a hand to wipe them away.

There are some things you learn best in calm, and some in storm.

~ Willa Cather

Gabby

Sam is in the ICU, so I can only go in for brief visits.

The first time, I can do nothing but stand by the side of his bed, not touching him, not speaking. To anyone looking on, I am a statue, an emotionless bystander with nothing to offer the man lying unconscious before me.

But on the inside, I am being shredded into a thousand different feelings, and letting any one of them out will surely mean I won't be allowed to come back in the room again. What I want to do, what I need to do, is scream for him to wake up, to tell me none of this is true. That everything is going to be fine.

But he can't. And when my time is up, I walk with my blank face to the nearest women's restroom where I lock myself in a stall and sob until I can't breathe.

I stay in the rest room until I have myself under

control again. I resolve to make my time in Sam's room about him and not me. And so, during the next fifteen-minute visit, I talk about things we used to do, friends we used to hang around with, hopes, dreams. Every good thing I can think to voice aloud, I do.

When I leave the room, I sit in the waiting area and think about the next time I go in and what I can give to Sam. Making this about me will take more from him. He's already had so much taken away. I will give him everything I have to give. What else can I do?

We came into the world like brother and brother;
And now let's go hand in hand, not one before another.
~ William Shakespeare

Gabby

I have been at the hospital for twenty-six hours when Ben gets off the elevator just outside the ICU. Our gazes meet in instant recognition. I stand, and he walks over to me, his expression heavy and tired.

"I would have recognized you anywhere," he says. "You haven't changed."

I shake my head in disagreement, but say, "Thank you. How are you, Ben?"

"Glad to finally be here," he says. "How is he?"

"He seems peaceful. Not in pain."

"I stopped downstairs to find out when I can meet with Sam's doctors. The administrator gave me this."

He pulls a folded piece of paper from his jacket pocket. His name is written on the outside in Sam's handwriting. "What does it say?" I ask softly.

"I haven't read it yet. I guess I'm a little afraid to." He

unfolds the paper, holding it where I can see it. It's only a few paragraphs. He starts to read.

Dear Ben,

If you have been given this letter, then I know something has happened before your return from Hawaii. I've known about my illness for several weeks now. It took a bit for me to decide how I felt about it, how much I was willing to do.

It's a little ironic, I guess, that I've ended up with the very thing you spend your days battling. But truthfully, there's no other hero I would want on my side than you. Once I learned about the trip you had planned, I decided to wait until you returned. I didn't want to deny you and your family that time together.

Honestly, even with your incredible skills, I know my case is on the fringes of surgery even being an option. I've been told it's unlikely that the tumor is malignant, but because of the size and location, removing it might mean that I will lose most of my memories, possibly have to learn how to walk and talk again.

You know me, Ben, and the thought of basically starting life over again as someone other than who I am, well, that's not something I want to do. I trust you to evaluate my case and make the decision you believe I would want you to make.

I rewrote this letter a few days ago. Unbelievably, Gabby and I have found each other again, but I know I have been cruel to her for opening a door I had no right to open. I've been too much of a coward to

tell her, and maybe selfish too. The time we've had together has restored my belief in the fact that we really do have soul mates in this world. She is mine. If I can't be who she fell in love with, that's not a person I want to be.

I love you, brother. Be the incredible doctor that you are in making this decision. If I'm not fixable, let me go.

Sam

I can't look at Ben for a full minute after he closes the letter. I stare down at my clasped hands, my chest tight with pain. He reaches over and covers my hands with his. I glance up and see his eyes liquid with an agony I can only imagine he must feel as Sam's brother.

"I haven't seen the scans yet," he says, "but I will have to honor what he has asked of me."

I nod once, but I can't hold back the sob that escapes my throat. Ben puts his arm around me and pulls me close. "I'm so sorry, Gabby. I'm so sorry."

"And I am for you," I manage to say. I look up at him then, force my gaze to his. "Can I just say that I understand what Sam has said about how he might be affected by surgery? But for me, I don't believe that removing a tumor can steal what's in a person's heart, can change the soul of who they are. I know Sam's heart and soul. And those are the things I love him for."

Ben puts his hand to my face and says, "I will do everything I can, Gabby."

"Thank you, Ben. I know Sam trusts you completely."

Ben stands and says, "I hope I can live up to it. I'll be back to let you know something as soon as I can."

As I watch him walk away, I can only imagine the weight of responsibility on his shoulders. He must make decisions like this every day, but with the distance of objectivity and professionalism.

His love for his brother will be a double-edge sword. It is a terrible place to be.

The greatness of a nation can be judged by the way
its animals are treated.
~ Mahatma Gandhi

Kat

I've been at Annie's house for a full day when I suddenly remember Sam's cat. I tell Annie about him and ask her if she'll drive me over to Sam's house to check on him.

Annie is one of the nicest people I've ever met, so we're in the car within five minutes.

When we pull into the driveway, there sits Eli on the front step in the same statue pose he'd been in the day we got back from Duke.

I get out of the car, careful not to twist my back, and walk slowly over to him. Annie follows me, saying, "Do you think he has food and water?"

I reach down to rub Eli's back and say, "Maybe on the side porch?"

I pick him up, and we walk around the house to the porch where the door is held open with a flower pot.

There's still plenty of food and water in the two bowls next to a table, so he hasn't been hungry or thirsty.

"He must be lonely here by himself though," I say, rubbing Eli's neck and hearing his instant purr.

"We could take him back with us," Annie says. "Just until Sam gets home."

"Could we, Annie?"

"Of course we can. I bet Sam would like knowing Eli has some company."

"I think he would too."

"Then that's what we'll do."

"Do you have any kitty food?"

"We can stop at the store and get some. How's that?"

I nod, and we get back in the car. Eli curls up on my lap, still purring. "You were lonely, weren't you? Sam will be back soon. We'll take care of you until then."

You are so brave and quiet I forget you are suffering.

~ Ernest Hemingway

Gabby

I drive home to take a shower and change. It feels as if I have been wearing the same clothes for weeks.

The house is depressingly empty without Kat here. I get in the shower and stand under the hot spray for a long time. I lean against the tile wall and close my eyes, wishing that I could climb into bed, go to sleep and wake up to find that this is all just some horrible nightmare.

But it's not.

It's real.

I get out and towel dry, putting on my robe and brushing my teeth. I wash my face and put on some moisturizer, wiping the steam from the mirror to stare at my reflection. I see a broken person staring back at me. And I realize that I'm already letting myself believe that Sam isn't going to live.

Desperate for something to hold onto, I open up the trunk in my bedroom. It sits at the foot of my bed, and it's where I keep things that are meaningful to me. Notes from Kat. Photos of us and things we love to do together. And my letters from Sam.

I never threw them away. I don't know why because when Sam married Megan, and it became clear that we weren't ever going to be together, it would have been the normal thing to do.

But I could never bring myself to do it. Instead, I stacked them up and tied them with a ribbon and bow, choosing to keep this part of what we'd had in a way I could keep nothing else.

I untie the bow now, pull the top letter from its envelope. It is from the first summer we met. Sam's dad had stopped their boat at our marina for gas. Sam left this note for me a few days after that.

Gabby,

You are the prettiest girl I've ever seen. Would you like to take a picnic with me tomorrow afternoon? My dad has said I can use the boat. I will come to the marina at one o'clock. If you don't want to go, I will simply be the goober there getting gas. But I hope you do.

Sam

I smile at this memory. Remember how nervous Sam

had been when he pulled up to the dock that day, how he'd dropped the tie ropes into the water and had to jump in after them.

His face had been three shades of red when he'd pulled himself back onto the dock and finally secured the boat, dripping water as he turned to me and stuck out his hand. "Hi, I'm Sam Tatum."

"Gabby Hayden," I said, smiling.

"Off to a great start, aren't I?" he said with a grin.

"Actually, you are," I said. "A lesser guy would—"

"Pretend he was someone else and drive off into the sunset?"

"Something like that," I said. "But it wouldn't have worked. I already knew who you were."

"You did, did you?" he asked, smiling bigger with the realization that I had noticed him the other day too.

"You're hard to miss," I'd admitted.

And I think from there, he lost the last of his embarrassment, because it was clear I liked him anyway.

The next several notes are from that same summer. Through each one, I relive how much fun we had together, parking the boat in a secluded cove and talking about everything we'd ever thought about. Finding time and again how much we had in common. We couldn't spend enough hours together. My whole world revolved around him.

It was at the end of our junior year when Sam's

parents told him of their plans to move to South Africa for his father's job.

Dear Gabby,

I don't want to eat or do anything that involves living without you. It's crazy that we'll have to live apart. Life without you is like the sky being gray all the time. The sun can't possibly shine through. What if we run away and get married? I know our parents would be mad at us, but they don't understand how this feels.

I love you so much, Gabby. Promise me we're going to be together one day. To know that is the only way I can live through this time without you.

Sam

I remember what I had written back as if it were yesterday. How I told him I would be miserable without him, and what I wanted was to go somewhere, any place where we could be together. But we were both scared of disappointing our parents, of not being able to support ourselves, and so we had promised each other we would get through it.

Waiting for Sam to leave felt like waiting for a death we both knew was coming. I realize now that I am feeling this exact same thing as I sit here reading his letters. Fearing the loss of him. Unable to imagine life without him.

I put away the last of them, tie them up with their red bow and place them back in the corner of the trunk.

All those years ago, I was helpless to stop Sam from leaving. Fighting the reason we were being separated would have done no good. But that's not true this time. However he is here, I want him. I love him. I have never stopped loving him. Somehow I have to make sure he knows that.

We must accept finite disappointment, but never
lose infinite hope.

~ Martin Luther King, Jr.

Gabby

At the hospital, I find Ben waiting outside the ICU. His face is drawn with worry and something that looks like resignation.

"Can we talk, Gabby?"

"Yes," I say, unable to hide my apprehension. I follow him to a small room with a few chairs and a table in the middle. He closes the door behind us and turns to look at me.

"Let's sit down," he says, pulling a chair out for me.

"Please," I say. "Tell me, Ben."

He sits down beside me, leaning on the table with his head in his hands. "It's not good, Gabby."

"Can you help him?"

"I believe I can remove the tumor. But the outcome is likely to be what Sam has already been told. Loss of memory, language, some motor skills."

"But he can live?"

"I believe so. Just not as the Sam he is now."

Tears well up and fall down my face. "Will you do it?"

"Gabby, I want to. I would do anything for my brother. But because of what he has asked of me, I need to know that I have his blessing. If I turn him into something he doesn't want to be, I'm not sure I can live with that."

"What are you saying?"

"I want to lessen the pain meds to the point that he is aware. I'll tell him what I want to do. And let him make the final decision."

"But what if he won't agree to it?" I ask, my voice breaking in half.

Ben presses his hand to mine and says, "Then out of love for him, we're going to have to accept that."

When life seems hard, the courageous do not lie down and accept defeat; instead, they are all the more determined to struggle for a better future.

~ **Queen Elizabeth II**

Sam

The fog is lifting. I've been submerged in it. Unable to see beyond its thickness. But now I feel it thinning, awareness descending, the lights in the room, the pillow beneath my head, the muted sounds somewhere beyond where I am.

As my mind starts to clear, pain begins to creep back in. A dull throbbing at first, muted, but there. The more awake I am, the more intense the pain. And when I finally open my eyes to try to see where I am, my head feels as if someone has inserted a knife into my skull, twisting the blade right and left.

"Sam?"

I struggle to place the voice. Ben. It's Ben. I force my eyes open, struggling to focus.

I see my brother standing next to the bed. His face is a

mask of sorrow and fear. I try to speak, manage to force out, "Big brothers aren't supposed to be scared."

"Yeah, well, right now, I don't really want to be the big brother."

"I know," I say, my voice barely audible. "It sucks."

I feel someone take my hand. I shift my gaze to the other side of the bed. It's Gabby. Her face is the same as my brother's, and I wince with the realization that I have caused this. "Gabby—"

"Shh," she says. "Just listen, okay."

I nod a little and blink with the determination to stay awake.

"I need for you to know something," she says.

I wait in silence, because I can't find the energy to speak.

She leans in close, her voice soft and pleading. "Sam. Fight. Please. Fight. For you. For your children. For us. Whatever happens, I'm yours. I've never wanted to be anything else. Let me be here for you. Fight this, knowing that whatever happens, I'm going to love you. And not even you leaving this world is ever going to change that. Stay here with me. Whatever you have to face, we'll face it together."

She breaks off there, kisses me on the cheek and says, "Please, Sam. Don't go. Please don't go."

I squeeze my eyes shut, managing a broken sounding, "I don't want to, Gabby. But if I stay, I won't be me."

"We'll rediscover you together," Gabby says, "like when we first met."

Tears well up, and I'm powerless to hold them back. "Gabby—"

She leans over and puts her arms around me, her head on my chest. "Don't leave me again, Sam. Please." She's crying now. I think of all those years ago and how many tears she must have shed for me. And I want to stay. I want to try. To fight with everything I have in me to come out on the other end of this battle.

I rub my hand across her hair, closing my eyes for a moment to reach for the strength I need to tell Ben what I want. I look at him then, my brother who is crying too.

"There's no doctor in the world I would take this on with except you, Ben. And whatever happens, just know that I will know you did everything that could be done. No guilt if it goes wrong, or if the outcome isn't what we hope. Can you promise me that?"

Ben nods, looking down at me with eyes filled with love. "Yes, Sam. I promise."

Selfishness is one of the qualities apt to inspire love.

~ Nathaniel Hawthorne

Gabby

As soon as Sam's pain medicine is increased, and he slips out of consciousness, Ben and I leave the room. I try not to listen as he calls Sam's children to tell them what is happening. They are both flying over from London on the first available flight.

"Are they okay?" I ask Ben, once he ends the call.

"Pretty devastated," he says, shaking his head. "They had no idea."

"Sam didn't want anyone to know."

"No. It's not hard to understand. He probably needed some time to figure out what he wanted."

"Thank you, Ben," I say, my voice breaking. "For everything you're doing."

"I just hope it's enough," he says, glancing down at his hands, as if he's questioning their ability to carry through with saving Sam's life.

"No one will try harder for him than you, Ben."

"I'd like to thank you, Gabby. If you hadn't come back into Sam's life, I'm not sure he would be willing to take this chance."

"Is it selfish of me? To ask him to go through this?"

"We're all selfish when it comes to holding onto the people we love. I don't want to let him go either."

I leave the hospital at just after two, driving back to the lake on winding Windy Gap Mountain Road, worries flashing through my brain like strobe lights, each one more blinding than the other.

I drive straight to Annie's house. When I pull into the driveway, she walks out to meet me. I get out and walk into her arms for a hug.

"Tell me," she says.

And I do, the possible outcome of Sam's surgery, my pleas with him to fight, even though I knew he'd already made up his mind not to.

"Was I wrong to do that, Annie? What if it doesn't work, and his agony is only prolonged?"

Annie leans back and tucks my hair behind my ear. "He's got one of the best neurosurgeons in the country. And it happens to be his brother. It seems like a gamble worth taking."

"But if he's suffering—"

"No battle like this is going to come without some measure of that. But if Sam made up his mind to take it on, he's strong enough to handle it."

"Oh, Annie," I say, my voice breaking.

She pulls me into her arms and holds me like my mother would have, just giving the comfort she knows I need.

The front porch door opens, and Kat walks out to meet us, her steps stiff.

She joins our hug. I kiss the top of her head and say, "How are you, sweetie? I've missed you so much."

"I missed you, Mama. How is Sam?"

I consider what to say, but then realize that she needs to know the truth. "He's really sick right now. But his brother Ben is a surgeon, and we hope that he'll be able to help Sam."

"What if he can't?" Kat asks, looking up at me with worried eyes.

"I believe he will. He loves Sam very much."

"We went to his house and picked up Eli. Annie said he could stay here too."

"That was really nice of you both." I look up at Annie then and say, "I'd like to go to Baltimore for Sam's surgery tomorrow. Ben wanted to do it at Johns Hopkins, and Sam is being transferred there. Would it be all right if Kat stays with you a little longer?"

"As long as you need her to. She's a joy to have here."

"Is that all right with you, Kat?"

"Do you want me to go with you?" she asks.

"I think it will be better for you to stay here and keep up with your schoolwork. I'm not sure how long I'll be there. Maybe we could run home and get you some more clothes and your school stuff."

Kat nods, and says, "Will you close the marina while you're gone?"

"I called Myrtle before I left the hospital. She said she and Timmy will be fine keeping it open."

"I could go over and help during the day."

"Thank you, honey. Let's see how it goes." I look at Annie and say, "I'll bring her back after supper if that's okay."

"See you then, sweet pea. I'll keep Eli company until you get back."

I open the car door, then look back at Annie. "Thank you," I say.

"For what?"

"Being my friend. No matter what."

"That's what makes it a friendship," she says. "The 'no-matter-what' part."

In the end, it's not the years in your life that count.
It's the life in your years.
~ Abraham Lincoln

Analise

The flight is completely packed. And we're in coach. The only seats we could get at the last minute.

I hate coach. No, I abhor coach.

Evan, on the other hand, is oblivious. He can sleep anywhere. Even in this ridiculously small, made for mini-humans, seat.

The flight attendant comes down the narrow aisle with the drink cart. I do my best impression of a twenty-one year old, order a rum and orange juice and promptly get carded.

"Nice try," the attendant says with an irritatingly cheerful smile, as if she's made it her life's work to nail minors looking to cheat the system.

I stare at the window and try not to roll my eyes. Anger crawls along my skin with an itch worse than the hives I had after a reaction to peanuts when I was ten. I have never been so mad or so scared in my life as I am right now.

I elbow Evan to wake him up.

"Huh?" he says, sitting up and rubbing his eyes. "What did you do that for?"

"How could Daddy do this to us?"

"Analise," he says, in the tone he uses when he thinks I'm being ridiculous. "I don't think Dad is doing anything to us."

"Why didn't he tell us?"

"I've never had a doctor tell me I have a brain tumor, so I'm not going to act like I have any idea how I would handle that news."

"I hate your practical nature."

"I've been hated for worse."

"And how could Mom not come?"

"They're not married anymore, Analise."

"At one point in her life, she loved him enough to make us. How do people just divorce each other and not ever care again what happens to the person they used to love?"

"We could ask Dr. Phil."

"Shut up."

"It's not Mom's place to be there. It's our place."

"And who is this Gabby person that Uncle Ben said called him about Dad being in the hospital?"

"Dad told me about her one time. When I turned

sixteen. We had a talk about girlfriends. They used to date when he was that age."

"Why have I never heard of her?"

Evan shrugs. "Because you're judgmental and—"

"I am not," I interrupt, smacking him on the arm.

"Okay," Evan says. "Whatever."

"Did he love her?"

"Yeah. He said he did."

"Why did they break up?"

"She lived at the lake where Dad's family spent the summers. When Grandpa had to go to South Africa for his work, they broke up."

"Because of Mom?"

"Apparently."

"So do you think that's why he went to Virginia without telling us? Because he wanted to see her."

Evan shrugs and looks out the window. I start to think he's not going to answer when he finally says, "Finding out that you might have a terminal brain tumor would probably make you want to tie up some loose ends, if you had any."

"And she's Dad's loose end?"

"When I talked to Uncle Ben, he said that — Gabby — would be at Johns Hopkins for the surgery too. So I guess we'll get to meet her there."

"I don't want to meet her," I say, pressing my lips together.

"Grow up, Lise."

"Shut up, Ev."

He looks at me and sighs. "Can we pause for a moment of maturity?"

"Whatever."

"You know Mom and Dad weren't happy for a long time."

"How would you know? Once you got your driver's license, you were never around."

"Yes, I was."

"No, you weren't."

"Okay, let me know when you're out of primary school."

I fold my arms across my chest and fume at him.

"You can keep your head stuck in the sand about what really happened between Mom and Dad or take a look at the actual truth."

"Dad worked all the time, and Mom got bored."

"She definitely got bored," Evan says.

"What do you mean?" I ask, frowning.

"Right after I first went to college, I came home one afternoon during the week to pick up a few things. I didn't call first. And Mom was . . . entertaining."

I lean back and give him a narrow glare. "Who? A man?"

"Yeah, a man."

"Did you know him?"

"No, but I doubt I would have recognized him with his clothes off."

"You walked in on them?" I ask, my voice rising.

"The living room couch was their spot of choice. It wasn't exactly something I could avoid."

"I don't believe you."

Evan leans back and closes his eyes. "Keep living in Neverland then, Lise."

I stare at my brother's clenched face, shaking my head. "Why didn't you ever tell me?"

"Because I didn't want to be the one who made you open your eyes where Mom is concerned."

"So why are telling me now?" I ask, my voice rising.

He lifts his head then and looks directly at me. "Dad's been wearing the black hat in your eyes for a long time. Maybe I just think you should give him a break given the shit deal he's currently facing."

Evan's words are harsh. He's never spoken to me like this, and I feel tears well up. "I didn't know," I say.

He studies me for a moment, sighs and reaches for my hand, taking it between his the way he used to do when I was a little girl and got scared about something. "Just let up, Lise. You've punished him enough."

Now that I've let the tears out, they won't stop, and I taste their saltiness on my lips. "Is he going to be all right, Evan?"

"I really don't know."

"What if he's not?"

"Let's not go there, okay? Uncle Ben is the best at what he does."

I know this is true. I've read the many articles Dad has saved about him throughout the years. I know how proud he is of his brother. But what if he's not good enough to save my daddy?

"I've been so awful to him, Ev."

"I haven't seen him much during the past year," he says. "I've been so caught up in my own world that I didn't call as much as I meant to."

"Sounds like we both need a second chance."

"Yeah."

"What if we don't get it?" I ask softly.

"Then I hope we can figure out how to live with it."

The tragedy of life is not that it ends so soon, but that we wait so long to begin it.

~ W.M. Lewis

Gabby

I leave home at four a.m. The first part of the drive goes quickly because there's almost no traffic. I stop for coffee a few times, but I can't eat. Just the thought makes me feel ill.

Outside of DC, the traffic starts to build, and I lose over an hour to constant starting and stopping. By the time I get to the hospital, my hands are shaking with anxiety. I've never been so glad to get out from behind the wheel.

I check the notes on my phone for the information Ben had given me on where to go. I ask for directions at the front desk and take the elevator to the correct floor. Ben had told me there would a waiting area outside the operating room and that I might be able to see Sam for a minute before they take him in.

I open the door to the waiting room. A young man

and a teenage girl are standing by the window, staring out. They turn at the sound of the door, and I realize they are Sam's children.

"Hello," I say. "I'm Gabby Hayden. You must be Evan and Analise."

"Yes, ma'am," Evan says. He walks over and sticks out his hand to me. His English accent, so different from Sam's, is startling. "It's very nice to meet you."

Analise walks over, her steps noticeably reluctant. "Hello," she says in a pretty English voice.

"Hello, Analise. It's nice to meet you too."

"Have you seen my dad?" she asks abruptly.

I lose my footing for a moment, but respond evenly with, "Not this morning, no."

"They wouldn't let us see him," she says, and her eyes go liquid with tears.

"I'm sure there's a reason," I say, my heart softening for the girl's pain.

"We got here over an hour ago," she says, "and we haven't even seen Uncle Ben."

The door behind us opens just then, and Ben steps into the room. "Hey," he says, his voice heavy with the weight of what he is about to attempt.

Analise runs across the room and buries herself in his arms, crying. "Uncle Ben, tell me he's going to be okay."

Ben closes his eyes for a moment, rubbing a hand across Analise's beautiful blonde hair. "I wish I could make you that promise, sweetheart. But I'm afraid I'm just the instrument. And I will do everything I possibly can to have the outcome your dad would want."

Evan walks over and Ben also pulls him into the hug. "Good grief, you two have grown up."

"Yeah," Evan says.

"You've both met Gabby then?"

"Yes," I say. "Just now."

"We'll be bringing Sam down the hall just outside this room in a few minutes. You can see him for a few moments then."

"How long will the surgery take, Uncle Ben?" Analise asks, her voice wavering.

"It depends on a lot of things, sweetheart. Expect a long wait."

He hugs them again and then walks over to hug me. "A nurse will call the phone in this room as soon as we're done, okay?"

I nod. "Thank you, Ben."

"I'll see you all in a bit," he says and leaves the room.

Once he's gone, the three of us are silent, and it feels as if we're trying to process all the possible outcomes.

"We should wait in the hall," Analise says. "So we don't miss him."

"I can stay in here," I say. "Give you some time alone with your dad."

"No," Evan says. "He would want to see you. And this needs to be about him. Not us."

It feels as if the statement has been made for Analise

as much as for me, and while I suspect she doesn't agree with him, she says nothing.

We wait in the hall for almost ten minutes before the elevator dings, and a young man with dark hair wheels a gurney out. I see Sam lying there, his eyes closed, his face pale.

"Daddy!" Analise cries out and runs to him.

His smile is weak, but he reaches out a hand to take hers. "Hey, sweet girl."

"Daddy," she says, and, like a child needing her father's comfort, leans over and hugs him tight.

"It's going to be okay, Lise. Please don't cry."

"Daddy, I'm so sorry . . . for being so awful to you." She tries to add something else, but her sobs won't let her.

"Analise. I love you, sweetie. We're good, okay. Whatever happens today, just don't ever forget how much I love you."

Evan stops at the other side of the gurney, taking Sam's hand in his. "Hey, Dad. I love you. You know that, right?"

"I know that, son. And I love you."

He looks up then and finds me. We hold each other's gaze for a long moment, and I let him see everything I feel for him. It doesn't need words. It never did.

"Ev and Lise, I need you to promise me something."

"What, Dad?" they ask in unison.

"That if I'm not around after this, you'll take care of each other. Be kind to each other."

"Don't say that, Daddy," Analise says, crying harder now.

"Gabby," Sam says, "can you come here, please?"

I walk over to the gurney with my heart pounding in my throat.

"There's one more thing I want you both to know, Ev and Lise. If I wake up from this, and I don't remember certain things, I need for you to know that I love Gabby too. I don't know whether we'll ever get to be together or not. Whether I'll wake up or not. But I love her. And I love you."

None of us is able to stop the tears streaming down our faces.

"Onward," Sam says to the man behind the gurney.

And as we stand there watching it disappear down the hall and through the doors marked "Surgery," I wonder how any of us will possibly survive the wait.

People seldom actually fit into our pigeonholes.

~ Author Unknown

Analise

I really don't want to like her.

I'm sitting across the room from Evan and Gabby, staring at my phone screen and acting as if I don't hear what they're talking about. Don't care what they're talking about.

A text comes through from Mom. I decide not to answer it. If she really cared about what is happening to Dad, she would be here.

Like Gabby.

"How long has your family lived at Smith Mountain Lake?" Evan asks her.

"My great-grandfather bought the land in the late 1800s. He had no way of knowing that some of it would later be turned into a lake, but lucky for my family, it was part of the Appalachian Power project, and we ended up with a lot of waterfront property."

"That's really cool," Evan says.

"Like most things," Gabby adds, "not too many people were for it in the beginning."

"I can imagine. What year was the lake started?"

"The dam was started in 1960. I think it took about four years to—"

"Will you stop?!!?" I bolt out of my chair, screaming, "How can you sit there and talk about stuff that doesn't matter in the least?"

Evan gives me a look and says, "Chill, Lise. We're just trying to make it through here."

"By talking about trivial crap?"

"Now you're being rude," Evan says, his mouth taking on a disapproving straight line.

"It's okay," Gabby says. "We don't have to talk."

Her tone is so nice and sympathetic that I instantly feel like the world's biggest bitch. "I'm sorry," I start, shaking my head. "It's just—"

Gabby gets up and crosses the floor to sit down next to me. She puts a hand on my shoulder and says, "You don't have to be sorry."

I start to cry outright then, great rivers of tears that make me feel as if I am drowning.

"Come here, honey," Gabby says, pulling me into her arms.

I resist at first, but honestly, her willingness to offer me comfort pulls me in, and I press my face to her shoulder, realizing I'm getting her sweater all yucked up. But she doesn't seem to care. She just holds me tight and rubs my hair, the way Mom used to when I was a little girl, and she actually seemed to like being a mother.

Evan comes over and sits down on the other side of me, patting my arm in the awkward way a brother does when he wants to show you affection, but realizes his cool factor is in jeopardy.

I stop crying eventually, my sobs becoming sniffs. But even after I do, Gabby keeps her arms around me. And I stay where I am. Because for the first time since Uncle Ben called and told us about Dad, I feel like someone else really gets how scared I am.

It’s not the straightest of lines — the walk between hope and faith.

~ Author Unknown

Gabby

We've been in the waiting area for almost nine hours when the phone on the small table by the door rings.

"Will you answer it, Gabby?" Analise says, her voice small and afraid.

I look at Evan and he nods once.

I pick up the receiver, my hand shaking as I say, "Gabby Hayden."

I listen as the nurse on the other end gives me the update we have all been waiting for. My heart initially lifts, wavers on its plateau and then dips again.

"I—thank you," I say. "We'll wait here for Dr. Tatum to come in."

I replace the receiver on the phone, closing my eyes for a moment before turning to face Analise and Evan.

"Your dad is out of surgery. But he will go from recovery to the ICU. They have him listed in critical condition. The nurse said your uncle Ben will be in to talk to us in a little while."

I see the effect my words have on each of them. They are feeling the same things I'm feeling. Gratitude that he has survived the surgery. Terror for what will happen from here. I sit on the chair behind me, feeling suddenly too weak to stand.

Both Analise and Evan come over and take my hands in theirs. And we all hold on to one another.

~

BEN WALKS INTO the room almost an hour later.

I don't think I have ever seen anyone look so exhausted. Fatigue hangs on him like a weighted coat.

Analise jumps up to hug him. He wraps his arms around her and squeezes his eyes shut for a moment. When he speaks, his voice is ragged with emotion.

"I was able to get almost all of the tumor. As we thought based on the scans, it appears to be benign, although it will still be biopsied."

"Oh, thank God," Analise says, crumpling against him.

Ben hesitates, as if having trouble getting out the rest. "I'm afraid he did experience a significant bleed though. He has a fight ahead of him over the next forty-eight hours or so. Let's just pray he's strong enough to get through it."

I stand and take Ben's hand in mine. "He will, won't he?" I ask, trying to keep my voice from shaking.

"It's up to him from here," Ben says, his eyes shadowed with worry.

"Can we see him?" Analise asks.

"Not for a while, sweetie," Ben says. "Let's give him some time, okay?"

"Okay," she says quietly.

Once Ben leaves the room, we each take our seats again.

Waiting, while Sam fights.

We can change courses, if we know the direction of the storm.

~ Author Unknown

Gabby

I'm alone in the waiting room. It's been three days since Sam's surgery.

Analise and Evan left a couple of hours ago to go to their hotel and try to get a little sleep. I told them I would call if anything at all changed.

The door opens, and Ben walks in. My heart throbs with painful expectancy. He still looks so tired. It's as if he's siphoned off much of his own life force in an attempt to infuse Sam with it.

Please don't let him be worse. Please don't let him be worse. The words pound through my head with the beat of a heavy drum.

Ben says something, and I shake my head a little, not sure if I heard correctly.

"What did you say?" I ask.

"Sam is awake."

I drop onto the chair behind me, my legs unable to support me. "Oh, thank God. Thank you, Ben. Thank you."

He comes over and sits down next to me, putting his arms around me and pulling me to him. "I thought we were going to lose him, Gabby."

"I know. I could see it in your face, even though you were trying to hide it."

"I did my best to stay objective, but he's my brother. And I love him."

I nod, crying now as I have not let myself in the past few days. It felt as if crying would mean I had accepted that Sam wasn't going to win the battle. Now that I've started, I can't stop.

Ben rubs my hair and lets me cry. I suspect he would like to do the same. Probably needs to do the same.

He starts to say something, then stops, as if he can't figure out how to say it. "Gabby . . . he . . . Sam doesn't recognize me."

My heart drops. We had known it was a possibility, but I guess I have been hoping for a miracle. "Do you think . . . will it be permanent?"

"The memories can come back. Some of them. It's really going to be a matter of wait and see."

When I can finally breathe again, I say, "I've heard that it's only in nearly losing something that we can truly understand what we have. It's true. I knew I loved Sam. Knew that I had never loved any other man the way I love him. But I will never be able to explain the gratitude I have for this second chance we've been given to start over. If he'll have me, that's what we'll do."

"You'll take good care of him?" Ben asks, leaning back to look down at me. "He's going to need you, Gabby. He's going to need a lot of help for a while."

"I will do everything I can," I say.

"Would you like to see him?"

"It's okay?"

"Yes, I think it would do him good to see your face. But you have to be prepared for—"

"I want to see him, Ben."

"Come on, then," he says. I follow him from the room, my hands shaking.

Ben walks with me to Sam's room, but just outside, he says, "I'll let you two have some time alone. Be back in a few minutes."

I push open the door and step inside the room, closing it behind me.

Sam instantly opens his eyes. His left hand goes to the bandages around his head.

"Hi," I say, standing at the side of the bed. "How do you feel?"

He looks at my face, his eyes narrowed as if he can't quite place me.

"Do you know who I am, Sam?"

He doesn't answer for several moments, and then, "No. I'm sorry."

The answer hurts. I won't deny it. "I'm Gabby," I say. "Gabby Hayden. You know me. Knew me."

"I'm sorry," he says again with worry in his eyes. "Can you . . . open please the curtain? I like to see the blue wide sky."

Tears blur my vision as I cross the room to open the heavy drapes. Light spills across the bed. Sam's face breaks into a smile. He stares through the window, his eyes drinking in the sunny day beyond this room.

And I think that is as good a place to start as any. With a blue wide sky.

Sam

Epilogue

I have always loved the spring. It's as if the world around us has been reborn, the tiniest of buds popping from tree limbs, green with life.

If I had to compare myself to anything right now, that's what it would be. Spring. It feels as if I've endured the harshness of winter, and life has revived within me.

It's April, almost a year since my surgery. It's hard to believe that much time has passed or that I've reached the place where I am now.

I'm sitting outside under the budding apple tree in Gabby's front yard. Our yard, actually, I correct myself. After our wedding three months ago, we decided we would live here, leaving my parents' lake house for Ben and his family to use on visits, which I am thankful to see, have been frequent.

I don't know what I would have done without him, without Gabby and Annie. Without Evan and Analise too. I've wondered many times what it must have felt like for them to think I might never regain any memories of our history together. It hasn't all come back, but enough that at some point, I began to feel my connection with each of them. To realize that they weren't strangers to me.

For weeks after the surgery, during my time in the hospital, and after I returned to the lake house with a fulltime nurse, it felt as if I had been dropped into a world I didn't know. But with time and healing, things began to return, bits and pieces of my history.

Eli has been napping in a limb of the apple tree. He hops to the ground and then onto my lap, stretching for a back rub. I comply, and he rubs his face against my hand. Since the day I came home from the hospital, he hasn't been more than a few yards away from me, having appointed himself my full-time guardian.

I hear laughter coming from the kitchen now. Gabby and Kat are cooking, and from the scent following their giggling out the open door, Gabby has burned the pine nuts again. Kat and I have decided it's not a big deal really. We just buy extra when we go to the grocery store and stock them in the freezer. We do love to tease her about it though.

She comes out on the deck and waves at me. "Hey, you. Need anything?"

"You," I say in a voice I hope doesn't reach Kat's ears.

She smiles a beautiful smile. "Be right there."

She sticks her head back inside, says something to Kat, and then, closing the door, runs down the stairs and through the yard to join me under the apple tree.

"You rang?" she says, one hand on her hip.

"I did," I say, reaching out with my left arm to pull her onto my lap. Eli concedes the spot and retreats to the apple tree.

Gabby curls up against me, pressing her face to my neck and saying, "You smell so good."

"You smell like an Italian kitchen. My favorite."

She laughs. "Not the sexiest scent."

"Anything on you is sexy."

"Hmm. Would you like to go upstairs and follow through on that suggestive tone of yours?"

"Yes, actually, I would."

She leans in and kisses me, softly, and then with the hunger that never seems to get satisfied between us. I start to lift my right hand to the back of her hair, but it drops to my lap halfway up.

Still kissing me, she picks up my arm and wraps it around her waist, holding it there because I have little to no function on my own.

"It's not always going to be like this," she reminds me. "Ben said it will mostly resolve over time."

"I know," I say. "I'm not complaining."

"It has to be frustrating though."

"It's okay."

"You amaze me."

"You amaze me," I say, kissing the side of her neck.

"No, really," she says, looking into my eyes. "You've handled all of this with a patience I'm not sure many people could."

"I'm alive, Gabby. And I have you, and Kat and Evan and Analise, Ben and his wonderful gang. I've been given a miracle."

She leans her forehead against mine, and we sit like that for a bit. I haven't said anything I haven't said before, but it is sobering to consider how differently things could have gone.

The door off the deck opens, and Kat walks out, cupping her hands to her mouth and calling out, "It's almost ready! You two lovebirds coming up?"

"On the way, honey," I call back.

She does a curtsey for us and then pops back in the house.

"Actually, we've had more than our share of miracles in this family," Gabby says softly. "I still can't believe she doesn't need to use her wheelchair now."

"David did an incredible job."

"He did. It's just so wonderful to see her walking around without pain."

"I know," I say.

"She's so excited about Analise coming to visit in June. She's making a list of all the things she wants to show her around here."

"Analise is pretty crazy about her."

Gabby covers my hand with hers and looks deep into my eyes. "I was going to wait until tonight for this, but I don't think I can stand another moment of keeping it from you."

I lean back, worried now. "Are you okay?"

"Yes," she says, her eyes lighting up. "We are, actually. Okay, I mean."

"You and me?"

"Yes. And your baby and me."

It takes a few moments for her words to sink in. I blink once and then, "Are you telling me—"

"I am," she says, nodding, her eyes lit with happiness. "We're going to have a baby."

"Gabby."

"I know. Another miracle."

I turn my hand and press my palm to her still flat belly. "Oh, Gabby. I never thought we—"

"Me, either," she says. "You can't make any assumptions about where life is going to take you, can you?"

"No," I say. I slip my arm around her waist and pull her up close against me. "Come here, beautiful woman of mine."

"Um, I love that part."

"Which part?"

"The mine part."

"Me too," I say. We sit there in the chair together, kissing like we did when we were sixteen and everything in the world seemed possible.

Turns out, it is.

Coming Soon! Book Two in the Smith Mountain Lake Series: Pink Summer Sunset

About Inglath Cooper

RITA® Award-winning author Inglath Cooper was born in Virginia. She is a graduate of Virginia Tech with a degree in English. She fell in love with books as soon as she learned how to read. "My mom read to us before bed, and I think that's how I started to love stories. It was like a little mini-vacation we looked forward to every night before going to sleep. I think I eventually read most of the books in my elementary school library."

That love for books translated into a natural love for writing and a desire to create stories that other readers could get lost in, just as she had gotten lost in her favorite books. Her stories focus on the dynamics of relationships, those between a man and a woman, mother and daughter, sisters, friends. They most often take place in small Virginia towns very much like the one where she grew up and are peopled with characters who reflect those values and traditions.

"There's something about small-town life that's just part of who I am. I've had the desire to live in other places, wondered what it would be like to be a true Manhattanite, but the thing I know I would miss is the familiarity of faces everywhere I go. There's a lot to be said for going in the grocery store and seeing ten people you know!"

Inglath Cooper is an avid supporter of companion animal rescue and is a volunteer and donor for the Franklin County Humane Society. She and her family have fostered many dogs and cats that have gone on to be adopted by other families. "The rewards are endless. It's an eye-opening moment to realize that what one person throws away can fill another person's life with love and joy."

Follow Inglath on Facebook

at www.facebook.com/inglathcooperbooks

Join her mailing list for news of new releases and giveaways at www.inglathcooper.com

Made in the USA
Middletown, DE
16 May 2018